LUNA JOYA

THE FAST AND THE FURIES

SYN CITY SHIFTERS
🐾 BOOK THREE 🐾

MYSTIC OWL

AN IMPRINT OF CITY OWL PRESS

THE FAST AND THE FURIES

LUNA JOYA

MYSTIC OWL

THE FAST AND THE FURIES
San City Shifters, Book 3

MYSTIC OWL
A City Owl Press Imprint
www.cityowlpress.com

Cover Design by MiblArt. All stock photos licensed appropriately.

Edited by Lisa Green.

For information on subsidiary rights, please contact the publisher at info@cityowlpress.com.

Print Edition ISBN: 978-1-64898-418-1

Digital Edition ISBN: 978-1-64898-419-8

Printed in the United States of America

ALSO BY LUNA JOYA

The Legacy:

Tides of Time (Prequel)

Magic Touch

Killing Song

Heart and Seek

Flash Point

***

The Wicked:

Wicked Crown

Wicked Match

Wicked Grace

PRAISE FOR THE WORKS OF LUNA JOYA

"A witch and an FBI agent find love while solving a years-old murder in the wickedly delightful second paranormal romance in Joya's *Legacy* series. The anticipation is delicious, and the eventual romance is well worth the wait. This sexy love story will entice longtime paranormal fans and draw in new readers." — *Publishers Weekly*

"Passionate and heartfelt, *Wicked Crown* delivers! Step into the goblin realm where court intrigue mixes with page-turning plot, Joya's electric foray into fantasy romance." — *J.E. McDonald, author of the Wickwood Chronicles*

"A magical debut full of unique, complex characters, fabulous sisterhood and an adorable dog. Who could ask for anything more?" — *Felicia Grossman, Historical Romance Author*

"With fast paced, heart pounding, thrilling suspense and fantastic displays of supernatural powers, *Magic Touch* is a paranormal delight! The romance isn't anything to sneeze at either! There is romance echoing through time and scorching the present. Readers will feel the heat of instant attraction and the sorcery of levitating passions." – *InD'tale*

"*Tides of Time* was one of those reads that kept my hands locked around my e-reader and my butt firmly planted in my chair. This book promises witchy mystery and romance, and it doesn't disappoint." — *Evie Drae, author of Queer Romance*

"A HOT romance with excellent chemistry between the characters, and a paranormal aspect that was both intriguing and contained a unique spin on magical powers." — *Amber K. Bryant, Award-Winning Author*

"Highly enjoyable. I was engaged from beginning to end. I was delighted in the different ways the author chose to incorporate magic into the book. These characters were well written. I hope to read more about these witchy sisters! I loved the chemistry between Cami and Sam. A wonderful debut for Luna Joya." — *The Literary Vixen*

"*Killing Song* is the high-octane third paranormal romance in Joya's *Legacy* series. Joya holds the reader in her grip with action-packed intrigue and an expertly paced will-they-or-won't-they. The satisfying ending still leaves plenty of room for the series to continue; readers will be eager to see that it does." — *Publisher's Weekly*

"*Heart and Seek* is a powerhouse of political intrigue, magical secrets, and sexy characters... For readers who love witches flexing their magical muscle, who drool over an intricate plot, and who believe that a love match should always prevail over a power match – this is it! This is a fabulous read. What will the delightfully devious Luna Joya bring us next?" — *InD'tale*

"Joya sends out her *Legacy* series with an enticing fifth paranormal romance, *Flash Point,* that finds the five Donovan sisters working to defeat the demon Nymvyra once and for all. The emotional friends-to-lovers romance plays out as a tantalizing tug-of-war between Mina and Josh, while the multilayered suspense plot provides satisfying answers to series-long questions. Readers are sure to be pleased." — *Publisher's Weekly*

For all who have loved enough to risk loss.
What is grief, if not love persevering?

1

NOLAN

My office, my life—hell, my whole world—revolve around the one case I couldn't solve. Sure, I hide the murder board behind evidence from an open investigation so no one can see my failure. But I can visualize every pinned photo and paper scrap tacked to it. The entire office thinks I'm the carefree and cocky wolf marshal who's gunning for promotion. No one else searches for the murderer who killed the Tucker family and my brother because *everyone* thinks he did it.

I know better.

Lowell wouldn't have hurt his mate, Hazel Tucker. He certainly wouldn't have slaughtered her entire family. There's also the impossibility of how he couldn't have ripped himself apart. The wolf marshals deemed it outside their jurisdiction since Lowell was one dead shifter outnumbered by five murdered humans. The human police didn't care. My little brother—the only person who loved me despite my secrets—was just another dead monster to embody the horrors our community represents for them.

"Bankston," my captain snaps. "Daydream about your latest romantic conquest on someone else's time."

Painting a wolfy grin on my face because it's the cliché that's expected, I lean back in my creaking chair far enough that a human would tip over, lace my hands behind my head, and hit her with a super-smolder shifter stare. "You jealous, Zaleski?"

She rolls her eyes so hard that I'm surprised she doesn't strain something. "Don't flatter yourself. There's been another murder, and it's got your boy's M.O. all over it."

Shit. The coffee I pounded earlier sours in my gut. I straighten and go deadly serious in an instant. I'm working the high-profile serial killer case that's left a trail of dead shifters across the country. I can't tell if it's a career-making opportunity or a curse. "The vic in this one?"

"A couple of deer shifters." She raises a hand to keep me from popping off questions. The captain knows me too well. "I realize the vics aren't predators so they don't fit your profile, but it's your guy."

Every major pack and possible power player in the shifter world has been hit—starting with my brother's murder—but none of the victims came from prey species. "How do you know it's the same killer?"

Her face goes green around the edges. "The vics were torn apart."

The same as Lowell and his fiancé's family had been. I fight the urge to glance toward the covered board. "What else can you tell me?" I don't bother with notes as I'll review every report, every photo, every witness interview I can get.

"It went down less than twenty miles from where that bobcat shifter murder happened two weeks ago," she says. "Predator then too. Not a pack leader as your profiling mentioned, but that vic was a well-respected elderly female. The dead deer shifters were the daughters of the herd's buck. Both fall under your category of vics whose loss would be considered a devastating blow to the community."

A devastating blow to the community. Lowell's death left one of the biggest wolf packs without leadership when the resulting shock ended his father's rule.

His father.

Not mine.

Not that anyone outside our family knows *that* dirty secret. It would ruin us all. Without the alpha, factions sprang up, internal wars erupted, and the entire city suffered for it. "So either this is a copycat murder," I say, "or our perp's narrowing the killing field geographically."

The captain shakes her head. "Your boy's slipping. Mistakes will make it easier for you to finally catch the bastard. The local authorities don't have the resources for this so I'm sending you to represent HQ."

I start gathering what I'll need for the trip—reports, recorder, spare batteries and phone signal boosters since electricity and connections are spotty everywhere outside the big cities where humans, shifters, and magic slingers cohabit peacefully. Allegedly. No one likes to talk about prejudice when infrastructure like power, water, and sewer rank so much higher. "Where?" I ask.

"Syn City."

No. Dropping into my seat, I try to keep my expression neutral, pulling out the poker face I've used to clean the meager pockets of patrol and lockup officers at five-card stud. But it doesn't work on her, and I don't want to explain why I have absolutely zero desire to visit the entertainment mecca of the supernatural world. "Their syndicate doesn't allow shifter law enforcement." Or any law enforcement outside some crazy winged avengers who are mortal daughters of Furies—as in Greek mythological legends come to life. "No way will they let me stay there." *Gods, I hope I'm right.*

"Both murder scenes are in the backwoods of nowhere. You can't conduct a complex investigation while staying in some local yokel's barnyard. I called in favors and got you a diplomatic pass since Syn City closed their borders to all outsiders given their recent incident."

"Great." I can't very well blame my heinously bad luck at being allowed into a town I don't want to visit on some kids who almost died and a country music superstar's mysterious disappearance. The news blasted: *Country Music's Golden Boy Vanishes, Musician Hero Sacrifices Himself to Save Children,* and *Syn City No Longer Trusted to Keep Visitors Safe.* No one could've missed those headlines exploding in every media source the week before Syn City shuttered.

"Look at the bright side, no tourists means fewer people to get in your way."

My problem isn't the gawking sightseers there to watch roller derby and concerts. No, it's one of the stars—the younger sister of Lowell's fiancé and my once fated mate who I could never make mine. Sadie Tucker.

"Our Atlanta office can't house me?" I'm man enough to keep the whine out of my voice. Mostly.

"Atlanta isn't close enough. Besides, I hear Syn City has all the tech you could dream of. The magic there supposedly amplifies it."

Yeah, the deity cities always have the best toys. I scan my office, searching for any last-ditch plea to get out of this jam. "We can't trust Syn City's syndicate not to have their own agenda. Any hotel there will have zilch for privacy, and we can't risk the confidentiality of the victims—"

"Zip it, Bankston. You're going. That's final." She glances at the closed office door, and suspicion finally sparks that should've been spinning since she shut it on her way in. "I need you out of headquarters for a couple of weeks until the heat on your use of force investigation dies down."

Anger surges through me, bringing my wolf so close to the surface that I bet my eyes gleam golden. "That guy was about to kill a kid. I took him out so he wouldn't shoot the boy."

"A boy who was a shifter. You killed a human. The inter-species authorities aren't happy."

I want to tear apart the desk, to chuck it at the stupid council who dares question an emergency situation from the safety of their secure chambers. "I'll bet the boy and his family weren't happy about him being kidnapped and kept as some sicko's pet either."

She jabs a finger at me. "I'm not saying you're wrong. Just that you need out of the spotlight. Since you won't take a two-week vacation and no one else can work this case, go to Syn City and find the damn killer that's been terrorizing our kind for years. Solve it, and all this will go away. You'll be promoted and then *you* can deal with the politics."

"Politics are their own nightmare."

"Can be." Captain Zaleski, the woman who can outtalk anyone in our station, goes silent—so quiet that the ringing of phones, squeak of shoes, and slamming of doors boom loud in my shifter hearing. "Look, go to Syn City. The affiliate agency pass will get you access to whatever resources they can provide. Solve the case, come back, and enjoy your promotion. Just don't shoot anyone while you're there and, for the love of gods, don't screw any of their deity daughter darlings. Or the interspecies council and this use of force investigation will be the least of your problems. Got it?"

I nod because there's no other acceptable answer, and she leaves, closing the door behind her.

Syn City. I'm so screwed.

Following her to the door, I twist the lock as soon as she's gone—the lock that I never used until now to keep the rest of the station out.

I can't have anyone else seeing this.

Papers rattle and wheels scrape as I turn the murder board to reveal evidence collected from the Tucker home—a big farm-house just outside of town, the white clapboards framing the blue door and welcoming porch. I climbed those front steps often enough to know exactly which creaked.

The memory of stepping around the squeaks when I was the first to find the murder scene? It makes me nauseous. A young marshal, I'd rushed inside with my gun drawn in hopes of finding Lowell's killer. Or anyone alive.

Hope. It's such a silly, fragile thing.

On the murder board, a sketch of the house's floorplan covers half the space with drawings of where each victim went down. I trace my fingers over the green lines and circles meant to depict a garden. I can almost push past the station's stink of ink, stale coffee, and shifter sweat to imagine the clean scents of herbs, flowers, and freshly tilled soil.

The garden had been Sadie's favorite place. A green witch, she'd constantly had dirt under her nails and grass stains on her clothes.

I found Lowell's body first, next to trampled rows of her beloved mint, rosemary, and lemon balm. My brother had been naked with scraps of his clothes scattered through the wreckage of vegetables and ripped-up herbs. Which meant he died as a shifter and transformed after death. Running my fingers along the sketch, I force myself to remember each awful detail with as much objectivity as possible.

With the brutality of the attack, I almost didn't recognize Hazel, his fiancé. She went down halfway between my brother and the porch while running for the safety of the house. I figure Lowell had been protecting her as he always did.

When I'd climbed the steps, avoiding the creaky boards, I'd prayed to whatever gods might listen that Hazel's parents and her two sisters had survived. I found everyone but Sadie dead in the kitchen. Two larger X's and a small one in red marker on the sketch seem so inadequate to memorialize a family that'd been vibrant and cheerful. The Tuckers were humans who practiced healing arts and kitchen witchcraft that'd gained them the respect of humans, shifters, and magic slingers alike. When the magic-blooded retreated to their sanctuaries during the Witching Wars, people like the Tuckers were the only ones left who could heal hurts that needed spellwork and white magic rituals.

When I'd followed a blood trail to the attic, I had fully antici-pated that I would find Sadie's body next to the altar where the family kept their grimoire. Hell, I have no idea how she made it up the stairs with the amount of blood she'd lost other than sheer stubbornness. But she'd been gone.

The tides of grief drowned out the jealousy, regret, bitterness, and shame that had darkened every time I'd ignored her instead of risking real *feelings* for her. Resentment came so much easier than exploring why the Fates matched me with the awkward but beautiful girl who was too shy and innocent to have a liar like me as a destined mate. I'd done everything I could to drive her away rather than chance dragging her into my mess.

Switching from the floorplan sketch to the photo of Sadie posted on the board, I study her gorgeous perfection that had been completely out of reach when I lived one exposed secret away from losing everything. My hungry gaze devours the curve of her jawline that I longed to stroke, the dip above full lips made for kissing, her wide-set green eyes that seemed to see through me to the not-a-wolf beast no one can ever know about, and the straight blonde hair that my fingers itched to find out whether it was as silky as it looked. The love I could never deserve but who I mourned as the impossible who I could at least watch over and protect from a distance.

I failed her in even that.

Before her murder. Before she made a deal with whatever immortal Fury brought her back to life. Before she went from Nashville's most sympathetic murder victim to her family's suspected killer, depending on what source the reporters cited.

Now, Sadie's a roller derby megastar in Syn City who inspires kid's costumes and is the face of a cosmetics brand. While Sadie's new hometown celebrates the kind of superficial star power she has, popularity won't help me track a serial killer.

I shove the board back into its hiding space, only pausing long enough to rip off the evidentiary envelope full of crime scene photos. Our unfulfilled mating bond couldn't have survived Sadie's death, and my past's too complicated to let it muck up the present murder investigations.

Except, if I'm right and whoever tore apart Lowell has killed again and again, then Sadie's the only witness who lived—sort of. Which makes her the key to solving my case, getting her out of my head permanently, and letting everyone know that my brother was innocent.

She's timid enough that getting her help won't be a problem, and if she decides to make this even more difficult than the memories I'll already be dealing with, I have the ultimate bribe to force cooperation. Even if it means letting go of the last link I have to the woman who haunts my dreams.

2

SADIE

WHEN I ROLLER SKATE AT MY MEANEST, EVERYTHING ELSE disappears—my grief, my inadequacy, my inability to do the one thing I was created to do.

All I feel is rage.

Not the wrath that my immortal Fury mothers grant when they allow us the chance to avenge those who wronged us. No, this irritable crankiness that I embrace when slamming into someone and knocking them off the rink? It's my shield against the rest of those gods-awful *feelings* that threaten to erupt and leave me behind as a hollow shell.

"Way to go," my Fury sister calls. Kiva's not my blood sister because I couldn't save either of those. But my found family *gets* my need for violence, and while I don't fit in anywhere, I can almost pretend here in Syn City.

Hit, *smack*, elbow, *crunch*. I attack other roller derby players like they're manifestations of the invisible enemies that I can't touch. How can I avenge my family's murder—*my* murder—when the killer's already dead? I've failed this family as much as my last, and my sad little salvation has become taking out the other Houses on the track like a one-woman demolition crew.

The shrill tweet of a whistle has me stopping, not even retaliating against the Gorgon who got in one last shove after the long rolling *screech* meant the end of our makeshift jam.

"You really nailed me with that hip check." Tisia, the Gorgon who I'd been battling for the last lap, slaps my hand in a high five that sends me rolling. "Good for me that you're such a skinny thing. If you had Jupiter-sized junk in the trunk like your Fury sister over there—"

"Hey," Kiva interrupts, popping out her hip and smacking her butt. "Not everyone can have this booty."

"Or their own makeup brand." Tisia nods at me and points to her cheekbone. "How'd you make the swirly thing that looks like a whip in your eyeshadow today?"

I shake out my wings, releasing the tension from skating with them tucked. "It's all in a flick of the wrist." As a human, cosmetics had been my way to hide that I was the less-pretty sister. Now, I camouflage so much more behind eyeliner, glitter, and customized skates. "I can show you if you want."

"I'll take you up on that." She glances to the stands—the empty stands. Without screaming fans, blinding spotlights, the smell of popcorn and cheese dip, the stickiness of spilled soda on the floor, and its usual cheerful chaos, The Rink seems a hundred stories tall instead of six. "Gotta go. My shift starts soon. See you at the Hack and Ale later?"

"Save me a target." Because lobbing an ax at a bullseye before tossing back one of Tisia's special brews sounds amazing right now.

"I'll leave it up to you whether your sisters can bring their shifters."

I don't bother hiding my scowl. *Shifters.* Ugh, I can't stand them, and my two Fury sisters mated with shifters.

Laughing at my expression, Tisia rolls away, her Housemates following. Most of Syn City's shuttered since we don't have tourists to entertain, but the Hack and Ale's still open along with a few local hangouts. Otherwise, having this many deity daughters stuck in one town would be asking for trouble of the magical variety. Some people work puzzles or knit when they're stir crazy. We're more likely to strangle each other with supernatural strength and speed.

Kiva skates toward me with her dark wings streaking behind her, seemingly on a collision course to crash into me when she jabs her toe stop into the concrete to brake to a halt. I don't flinch. While I'm good on skates, she's amazing. "Must be hard being you, beauty queen," she says. "I can't imagine how many poor human hearts you broke before becoming a badass Fury."

I throw a mischievous glare her way instead of confessing the truth that no one in Syn City would believe. The only guy I ever liked? He treated me like a little sister. Not shocking since we met when I was eleven and he was almost nineteen. But when I had my fifteenth birthday? Almost overnight, he began ignoring me. Or worse, if I somehow *did* manage to attract his attention, it was to remind me that I was the weird girl in high school who talked to plants and didn't rate time with a wolf marshal.

I was looking for connection. He wanted nothing to do with me.

Worse, his brother and my sister had been together which meant he was at my house almost every friggin' day. Of course, that was *before* his wolf shifter brother went rabid and killed me and my whole family—including his fiancé and even my baby sister—only to off himself. The jerk who I'd crushed on, the high and mighty wolf marshal? He did his best to cover up my family's murder as if it'd never happened.

Screw shifters.

And screw my twisted brain for dredging up memories of Nolan Bankston and my family when Kiva had been trying to compliment me.

"You up for racing?" I ask her. "We might as well get some

speed work in. The House Cup challenge won't win itself when the crowds return."

Kiva dashes away. "I'll win."

I zoom to catch up with her. "Cheater!"

"Says the loser."

The clack of our skates on the track echo in the empty stadium, and I surrender to the whirring of wheels, Kiva's laughter, and my pounding heartbeat as I pour on the speed. Dizzying laps later, my Fury sister declares it a tie.

"Good thing our third wasn't here." I hold my arms overhead to slow my ragged breathing.

"Dottie would've smoked us both," she says.

True. Our other Fury sister is a speed demon. "We could've made it a wings-out round. She would've tripped over her big butterfly ones."

"Next time—" Kiva cuts herself off, looking up into the stands.

I follow her gaze. Bunny, the rabbit shifter who's in charge of maintenance at The Rink, stands next to the railing, much closer than she'd normally get when I'm here. It's not a secret that I don't like shifters. Although Bunny isn't a predator. I can't see the grey-haired, fast-talking rabbit as someone who'd go rabid and tear apart the people who loved her. Then again, no one had expected that of Lowell either.

"What's up, Bun?" Kiva asks.

"There's a wolf marshal here," Bunny says. She shifts her stance from one foot to the other as if the topic makes her as uncomfortable as it does me. "Says he's investigating the shifter murders and has permission to question anyone in Syn City who might have information."

Paranoia pricks at me, edging toward panic. A wolf marshal like Nolan? Impossible.

"Our Syndicate would never allow a wolf marshal here." My voice barely shakes and comes close to the certainty I need. We survive as a powerful city because our seven anonymous leaders known only by their collective name keep us above common supernatural power struggles.

"*Riiight*," Kiva chimes in. "The wolf marshals are barely more than a militia hiding behind badges. Did you know they allow immediate executions when a single marshal finds a suspect guilty of murder? So friggin' barbaric."

I can't help but point out the obvious. "Not that I have any respect for wolves, but we're Furies. *We* execute people."

Kiva gives a massive sigh. "Only when the immortal Furies tell us to. It's different. It's divinely ordained."

"Uh huh." I glance at Bunny. "Where's this marshal? Want us to throw him out for you?"

She stares at her feet. "Slaya, I mean, Sadie…"

"Yes?" I ask when she doesn't finish. Clearly, I've done too good of a job of scaring this particular shifter. I remind myself she's prey and likely to run or hide if my bark suggests I might bite. "It's okay, Bunny. Just tell me."

The scared rabbit still won't meet my gaze. "The marshal asked to speak with you specifically."

My stomach twists into a tangle worse than any knots in my skate laces. "Did he call me by my roller derby name?"

As a Syn City star, I'm known as Slaya to outsiders, and that's the brand on makeup, t-shirts, and other merch. As Sadie Tucker, true crime fans have defined me as an innocent exiled into a violent, revenge-driven existence to avenge my family's brutal murder. They consider it a real-life horror with a magical ending. Those idiots forget that I died, my entire family was slaughtered, and there's no one left for me to take revenge on.

"Nope." Bunny seems to shrink even smaller into her over-sized coveralls.

The knots in my stomach go sour and turn as heavy as stones. *Why would a wolf marshal want to talk to me?* A terrible thought spirals in my mind. Oh no. He wouldn't dare. "What's the marshal look like?"

She looks at me—full on meets my gaze—as though surprised I asked. "Tall, good-looking for a wolf with auburn hair and brown eyes. What he's wearing makes sense if he came from their Nashville headquarters, but if you want my opinion, he's a cocky S.O.B."

All the blood rushes from my head, and the sweat from our skating morphs into cold dread.

Nolan Freakin' Bankston's here in Syn City.

As if he didn't irritate me enough in my prior life, the man followed me here? And the Syndicate let him? Where are the mobs of fans when I need them to stand between me and the wolf whose brother murdered my family? I cursed myself by even thinking of him today, and the possibility of him being here triggers a landslide of memories when he ignored me, mocked me, or acted as if I didn't belong *anywhere*.

"Sadie." Kiva rolls closer. "You okay, beauty queen? You're looking a little pale. And green. Tell me you're testing a new concealer and that this isn't about the marshal."

"I know him. Or at least I did." My throat tightens around the admission.

"And do we like him?" she whispers.

Like—such a funny little word with so many meanings. I shake my head, unwilling to talk about my past more than I have to. I'm not that nerdy girl who's jealous of her big sister's looks and her baby sister's visions anymore. I'm the caged vengeance who's tired of being leashed. It's been three years—a literal lifetime ago for me.

"Want me to stay with you? Or go get my grizzly bear to help bury whatever pieces you leave of the marshal?" she asks. "Whatever you need, I'm here for you."

Thank the gods for the triads that the immortal Furies created. Our deity mothers gave me two badass friends who accept me no matter what. I don't deserve their love seeing as how I'm the Fury without revenge to reap, yet they continue to give it. "I'm glad we're sisters."

"Damn straight we are," she says.

"Get Stone." Her grizzly mate acts like a teddy bear around her, but he can shift into a terrifying giant. Besides, I don't need Kiva deciding to torment a marshal just because she can. "Grab our sister and her mountain lion if you see them." For once, I'm not bitter about being their fifth wheel these days. "As witnesses or backup or—"

"On it." Kiva takes to the air, not bothering to change out of her skates.

I can do anything with my sisters—even banish the bully of my past.

Bunny looks as though she's trying to hide under one of the stadium seats, twitchier than a meth addict. "Don't skin the messenger," she says with a squeak.

"I'll meet with him," I tell her. "Bring him in." On my track in my Rink with the home turf advantage. I straighten my spine and wrap cold anger around me like body armor.

Forget the recent outbreak of serial killers and crazy sea monsters we've had in Syn City. Hell hath no fury like an actual Fury, and Nolan will regret the day he decided to mess with this one.

3

NOLAN

BETWEEN THE RECON I DID AT MARSHAL HEADQUARTERS BEFORE THE trip and then the eternity that the damn rabbit shifter makes me wait outside, I should've memorized all seven Houses of deity daughters in Syn City. The Rink—yes, they insist on capitalizing it—stands six staggering floors, towering over everything else so that it's visible from miles away. A jumbotron dominates one curved side, but much like everything else in this town, it's dark. Banners for each House have been painted along the exterior columns. I stare at them, but I'm still having trouble remembering all seven.

The black banner stands for the House of Furies—Sadie's group. Which explains why she's only ever photographed in black.

The women who pushed past me a few minutes ago, glaring at me as if willing my dick to shrivel with a glance? Gorgons in yellow with snake tattoos. Fucking snakes.

Gods, I hate snakes.

The other Houses run together. Not that it matters when I'll sweet talk whatever I need out of Sadie in the next few minutes, gather evidence from the two crime scenes tomorrow, and leave this strange place that even smells wrong.

With the whole town empty other than deity daughters, their families, and staff employed by the Houses, the hotel in what they call their Pleasure District has closed until the tourists return. So I'm stuck in a small cabin at the edge of the woods next to a medieval weapons training school where the sound of women's war cries echo like there's a battle headed straight for my front door. Several of those women look as though they'd rather make out with a knight than become one themselves.

I got dropped off at the cabin by a Huntress and told *don't go into the woods or the Furies might toss you to the sea hags in the swamp, especially the blonde Fury who hates shifters.*

The sooner I get out of here, the better. Preferably if I can go without meeting that particular shifter-hating Fury.

Captain Zaleski can get the brass to lay off me for the use of force investigation if I bring them a suspect. Not that I understand them coming down on me for shooting someone who hurt a kid, but politicians love to brag about solved crimes, and stopping a serial killer means another press opportunity for them. They don't need to know it means the world to me.

The squish of work boots approaches, and I shade my eyes against the setting sun to see the rabbit shifter returning. *Bunny.* What self-respecting shifter lets herself be named after her animal? Her nose twitches to the point I wonder if it's a nervous tic or an affectation to mess with my head. Hell, it makes me want to scratch my face to get rid of whatever's bothering her.

"She agreed to see you," she says.

Thank the gods. "She alone?"

Not that it matters, but Sadie will be easier to manipulate if she doesn't have anyone else to hide behind. She could barely string a coherent sentence around me at her parents' house yet she'd stood up for her baby sister any time she thought I'd dared to insult the kid.

Shame, guilt, and regret roll through me. If I'd known there'd be a threat, I could've arranged marshal protection, and the little girl and her whole family would be alive. So would my brother. Shoving those still-open wounds aside, I scowl at the rabbit who's reluctant to answer me.

The twitching stops for a moment. "She's alone for now, but I'm coming with you."

Brave little bunny.

I follow her through the double doors. The massive coliseum looks like holograms I've seen of professional basketball arenas from the time before the Witching Wars. Stacked with seating on every concrete level reaching to the roof, it doesn't waste spectator space on an exterior loop. We enter on the middle round where concessions stands and merch counters crowd the space, casting shadows from the low lights above. With a quick glance at the ceiling and the maze of metal catwalks beneath it, I estimate only a quarter of the normal lighting's activated.

Bunny follows my gaze. "Without the tourists, we cut everything but the essentials to keep energy use down. Part of the Gorgon team practiced today."

Which explains the players who left earlier, but not the skater I'm looking for. "I thought Sadie was a Fury."

"She is. Best you not forget that." Without expanding on her cryptic comment, the rabbit walks ahead to the steep descending stairs toward the oval skating track below.

The track's empty. I inhale, pushing past the scent of the rabbit, the Gorgons who left, and harsh disinfectants. *There.* What is that perfume? It yanks me faster down the stairs until I almost topple over Bunny.

A woman stalks up a half-flight of steps that lead from the track to the stands. With her long blonde hair pulled into a sleek ponytail, she's dressed in black that skims over her curves. *Sadie.*

She turns her gaze on me, and my world narrows to her. My vision goes fuzzy at the edges, and a freaking gong beats in my chest where my heart used to be. I can taste the tartness of crisp apple and smell autumn leaves. A pull starts deep within my belly, a tugging of heavy chains and unbreakable ropes that lead back to the anchor of *her*.

No. That can't be. She died. Any fantasy I had of a fated mate died with her. After three years of being stuck unable to fantasize about anyone but her, with one locked gaze, my inner beast has chosen his mate. Death didn't destroy the bond. If anything, it's stronger now.

Mine, my wolf—mixed with the other animal that the marshals don't know about— screams in my mind. I could simply take her, force her not to reveal the secret that could destroy my career. I'm still deciding whether to give in to my beast's urge to grab her or run when she speaks.

"You're not welcome here, marshal." Her upper lip—that fullness that pillows bigger than the bottom one in upside-down lushness—curls into a sneer.

What happened to the sweet, timid girl who would hide from her shadow? "Your Syndicate says otherwise." I flash my badge and the written pass that mean I have as much right to be here as she does.

She keeps her gaze on my face. "I don't know what lies you told or who you had to screw to get that, but I'm not impressed."

I switch tactics. "Look at little Sadie Tucker all grown up." And damn did she grow up gorgeous. "Haven't you missed me?"

"Don't flatter yourself." She folds her arms over her chest which pushes her breasts up, and I wish the neckline went lower than the barest hint of cleavage. "Why don't you disappear for a few decades and see if I miss you then? Spoiler alert, I won't."

From my left, Bunny coughs to hide a chuckle.

It's time to remind them both how serious this situation is. "I'm investigating the murder of two local shifters."

"Not from Syn City, you're not. We aren't missing any." Sadie climbs the stairs toward me, her movements graceful. If I didn't know she'd been born human, I would think she's a big cat on the hunt. "And why would I care about a couple of dead shifters?"

I glance at Bunny, waiting to see her shock. When she simply stares ahead, I ask, "Did you not hear what she said about our kind?"

The rabbit shrugs. "She hates all shifters."

So Sadie's the Fury I was warned about who hates us. What happened to Hazel's sweet sister who spent more time with plants than people?

"Bunny's at least useful," Sadie says as she steps toe to toe with me. "Which is more than I can say for you."

I curl my mouth into a smile with no hint of niceness. "Don't tempt me to show you how useful I can be."

"As if you could tempt me." Venom drips from her voice with a huskiness, a throaty *sin incarnate* vibe.

The Sadie I remember puzzled me. *This* Sadie thrills me. My beast wants to make her ours, but that's not how mating works. The claim has to go both ways. Yet the tension building between us makes me want to wrap my fist around her ponytail and drag her face up for a kiss to prove how scorching this thing between us could be. "Oh little Fury, I promise you'd like it."

She unfurls two giant black wings that rustle the same as the flipping pages of a book. Symbols flicker over them as though writing and erasing blood-red ink to an inaudible beat. If I let my vision go hazy, it's a dark version of her family's grimoire, but the symbols look...wrong. I can't figure out exactly how even though I've stared at the book for hours since I stole it from the crime scene.

Bunny backs away. "All right then, I'll leave you two to it." With that, the rabbit takes off.

Sadie doesn't drop her gaze from mine. "Time to go, marshal."

"I just got here, and I like the view." I ease back on my heels. When her gaze goes dark, I know I've scored a point. "I thought you might be happy to see someone from your past."

"The man who abused his marshal power to try and keep my family's murder quiet?"

"I did it to protect you from headlines." Not that it worked when the media latched onto the horror of a shifter slaughtering an entire human family. Then, there'd been the magic-haters who'd suggested that Sadie had committed the murders in some evil pact with the immortals to become a Fury.

"I don't need your protection. If you made the trip to reminisce, then you wasted both our time." She walks by me, standing a step above so that we're eye level.

I catch her hand, trailing my fingers along her soft skin. It's the first time I've touched her in years, and with the way that slight contact sends electric sparks igniting both my beast and my human forms, I wish I'd found her immediately after her turn from human to mortal deity daughter. Her eyes go wide for a moment, and I wonder if she felt that buzz too.

"I have something of yours." I let my tone go flat, but I don't release her hand. "Help me with the investigation, and I'll hand it over to you."

"If it's mine, then I shouldn't have to earn its return. Give it back." Her sultry command almost has me reconsidering my selfish demand—almost.

"Not until you help me clear Lowell's name."

She yanks her hand away. "Your brother murdered us and then took the coward's way out by killing himself before I could take my revenge as a Fury."

"Don't tell me you believe Lowell could literally tear himself apart. Here I was thinking you'd gotten smart in this second life."

Hurt flashes in her gaze, and it leaves a hollowness in my chest that has my wolf howling inside. She looks away and I want to soothe the pain, but I don't because while I'm an asshole, I'm not enough of one to make promises I can't keep. And what the hell has she used on her eyes to make the skin around them sparkle like that? She has painted a spiral that winds from her eyelashes like the perfect replica of a coiled whip. Seriously, I can almost hear a crack in the air when she blinks.

"Whatever you have of mine," she says, "I can assure you it's not enough to make me help you." Damn, she says *you* like I'm the problem. It's hot.

Which will make it even hotter when I prove her wrong. "I have your family's grimoire."

She moves so fast that a whip unfurls in her hand before I see her reach for a weapon. *Shit.* I go for my gun, and the roar of a bear has me flinching enough to fumble on the draw.

On the mid-tier level where I came inside, an honest-to-gods grizzly bear stands on his rear paws, roaring as if he'll rip my throat out. How the hell did a Kodiak make it this far south? An impulse from my inner beast has me wanting to shove Sadie behind me, but she doesn't seem surprised by a bear being inside a skating rink. Or that two women drop from the air to the staircase behind her with full wings extended. Both wear black.

The shorter-haired brunette flips a hatchet in her hand. The other with massive butterfly wings holds fiery...what are those?

I stare and ask, "You going for a Grim Reaper look? Should I have come in costume?"

The hatchet wielder grins a smile so fierce that I would expect to see fangs if she was a shifter. "Let's see if you're still funny when we hack you to itty bitty wolfie pieces."

More Furies ready to kill me—just what I need.

4

SADIE

MY EMOTIONS PINBALL FROM ANGRY TO SAD AND BACK AGAIN. Nolan stole my family's grimoire three long years ago, and now he wants to bribe me with it to help *his* family?

"Your family *destroyed* mine," I remind him. "Seems fitting that my new sisters watch me destroy you."

Kiva flips her hatchet. "Sounds like we made it just in time for the party." She calls over her shoulder to her bear mate, "We've got it from here, honey."

My other sister, Dottie, lowers her flaming sickles and leans closer to me. "Did you get a telepathic kill signal from the immortal Furies?" she whispers. "Because you don't look all wrath-of-the-gods mad other than your weapon to call."

"What's a weapon to call?" Nolan asks as if I hadn't threatened him with death. "The fiery Grim Reaper things?" He raises his chin toward Dottie's weapons.

"No," I answer her question, ignoring his ass for a second the way he ignored me for years. While Dottie and Kiva have both been granted permission by the immortals to avenge their families, that won't be happening for me since there's no one left alive to blame. "And they're sickles," I say to Nolan because I would rather talk about petty trivialities than think about my traitorous body.

My heart's pounding, and I'm tingling in places that should not be lighting up like Syn City during the derby cup challenge week for this *dog*. When did he go from boyishly handsome to ruggedly hot? He means less than nothing to me so he shouldn't be able to hurt me with sniping comments or incite more desire than I've felt since.... since I crushed on him last time. No, I won't admit to anyone that I'm still a virgin. Least of all Nolan Bankston.

"What are sickles?" he asks.

And now I've lost my train of thought by staring at him instead of staying on topic. Why does he still have to be so good looking with broad shoulders that fill out his button-down shirt, a lean waist and muscles that make those worn jeans cling to him, and battered boots that look as though he could transition from a suspect interrogation to a ranch hand in a blink? Why couldn't he get old and ugly?

He props his hands on the belt where his holstered gun and a star-shaped badge hang as if *gunslinger cool* might be his usual stance. Dark red hair, whiskey-colored eyes, and a long, lanky frame complete the "hot cop" package. The jackass even smells good. I scowl because he distracted me with his stone-cold fox— er, I mean wolf—studly self.

"They're sickles. My weapon to call," Dottie explains. "The reaper carries a scythe."

"Missing the pole thing." Kiva wags her hatchet as if punctuating the point. "You should take your hand off the gun. Not so smart bringing a firearm to a Fury fight, marshal. Shooting a deity daughter would bring down a curse on you and your entire family. It's the reason our weapons to call come from the ancient armories—my hatchet, Dottie's sickles, and Sadie's whip."

He flicks his gaze to mine and shoots me a sly smile that

makes me want to punch him in his perfect teeth. "Good to know. I hadn't planned on shooting anyone."

"Should've left the gun at home," I say. "Like *you* should've stayed at home. Now, give me back what you stole from my family."

"First, tell me what you know." He doesn't seem to realize the danger of having three armed Furies in front of him whether or not we feel authorized to kill him by the immortals. We're trained in dealing out pain other than the deadly kind.

"About the local shifter murders? Zero." I flick my fingers in a *gimme* move. "The grimoire."

"Wait." Dottie touches my arm. "As in your family's grimoire? The one you were going for when…" She gestures toward my wings instead of finishing her question.

"When this asshole's brother murdered me?" I don't sugarcoat the truth. Why should I? To spare Nolan's feelings? He never showed mine any mercy. "The one I was scrambling to make it to when I died? Yep, that's the one he claims to have." I failed to reach the altar, to find the right protection spell, to save my family.

"We could toss him in the swamp," Kiva offers. "Let the sea hags have him."

Tempting, but I shake my head. "The water moccasins would scare him more, but dumping him in the swamp won't get back my grimoire."

"What will?" Dottie, ever the peacemaker, asks in her country twang.

"He wants help clearing his brother's name."

"Time out." Kiva nudges me with her hatchet's handle. "I thought he came here to investigate the shifter murders—not your murder."

I don't have an answer for her so I stare at Nolan which shouldn't be so easy to do. Marshals aren't supposed to be muscled with square jaws.

"The shifter murders and Lowell's are related," he says. "Every crime scene had arrowheads like those in your wings," he tells Kiva.

We all glance at the dangerous silver tips on Kiva's feathered wings.

"How'd he know they were arrowheads?" she asks me as if I have any idea. "I didn't know what they were until recently. I thought they were dagger pieces."

Nolan slowly holds his hands up, palms facing us. "If I reach into my jeans pocket, do you promise not to decapitate me?"

Kiva snorts a laugh. "If you flash us your pecker, the grizzly and the mountain lion at the top of the stairs will gut you where you stand."

"You have shifter mates?" he asks, and I'm pretty sure he's talking to her, but he stares at me.

"Yep." I don't offer more info. "Unless you have directions to my grimoire in your pocket, we're not interested."

"I think you will be." He pulls metal out of his pocket, rolling it through his knuckles like a poker chip before pinching it between his thumb and index finger. "Recognize this?"

It's a silver arrowhead like the one that killed Kiva.

"You found that at the shifter murders?" I ask, my voice sounding far off and flat.

Kiva had been human like all of us Furies in our first life, but she'd been killed in the company of her bear shifter mate moments after the murder of a shifter teenager. The girl had only been fifteen years old, but then my baby sister Mabel had been nine.

"We've found at least one arrowhead at every shifter murder." He loses the sarcasm. "But not this one." He grips the silver tighter.

When he leaves the rest of the explanation hanging unsaid, I bite. "Where'd you find that one?"

"In Nashville. At your family's house—"

"No," I say before he can finish. *Deny, deny, deny.* Because otherwise grief will spill out and carry me away on waves of pain that I won't survive. Not without a guarantee of the revenge I was promised.

"Oh, Sadie." Dottie's big butterfly wings droop.

Kiva goes on the attack, stepping around me and closing in on Nolan. "You might think you're the shit since you're a big bad wolf shifter but know that pack laws don't apply in Syn City. If you're lying to her, we'll dump your mangy butt in the swamp for the harpies, and no one would be the wiser."

"I'm not lying," he says. His gaze stays on me. "I was the first person on the scene, and I found this in the kitchen when I discovered your parents and your little sister..."

Their bodies.

Chills ratchet up my spine as violently as a full flight of Furies in battle rage. "My family didn't keep weapons." I push the words out through a tight throat and dry mouth.

"I know." He would, given how often he'd visited our home.

A single arrowhead doesn't prove anything, does it? "The detectives said Lowell went rogue, that he killed my sisters and parents before committing suicide. The wolf marshals confirmed that shifters can die of the same wounds that kills their fated mate. That it's extremely rare, but possible."

"They lied, and I need your help to uncover the truth."

What if he's right and whoever killed me and my family is still out there? What if they're terrorizing other families? What if I can finally have the sweet revenge that the immortal Furies promised me when they brought me back for another chance? "A random arrowhead is hardly proof of Lowell's innocence," I say. "Only a shifter could've had the strength to do what was done to my family."

"Or to the poor kid I was searching for when I died," Kiva adds quietly.

"This isn't just *any* arrowhead," Nolan says. "I had it analyzed at our lab and then asked a friend at a magical research archive to examine it. She says the carvings look like part of a bigger engraving—a possible invocation of a deity."

A deity? "Which god or goddess?"

Nolan shakes his head. "She isn't sure. She narrowed it down to a few contenders but none have known followings here on the continent, and no other countries have had the shifter serial killings."

"Are we sure it's not the Huntresses?" I ask my sisters, always looking for a reason to hate on our worst rivals. "They carry those bow and arrows as though their goddess outranks all of our immortal makers."

"They don't seem the type to tear people apart," Dottie points out, ever the voice of reason. "Outside of derby bouts, they don't start fights. Wouldn't this killer have a hard time hiding that kind of violence?"

I glance at Kiva. She hates the Huntresses as much as I do.

"Dottie's right," she says. "They're busier proving they're better than anyone else, but I asked, and Devlyn swore they wouldn't waste good silver for arrowheads. Or points, she called them. They're pretentious bitches, but they don't lie."

"Who's Devlyn?" Nolan asks.

"The Huntress's coach. Their leader." Heavy hurt weighs me down, and I feel like I've aged ten years in the last ten minutes. I can't do this right now. I banish my weapon to call since there's nothing tangible for me to beat down to release the tension. Not yet anyway. If the cocky asshole marshal's right, the fight that I've been denied for years might be coming.

The powers that flow through my veins call for vengeance to soothe the ten tons of guilt and sorrow I carry in my heart—the memory of my older sister calling Lowell's name. Yelling for her mate, her fiancé right before her screams stopped. Or my baby sister crying for me, for Mom, for anyone. I would give *anything* to banish the shame I carry at my failure to save them. Even work with the wolf who holds my grimoire hostage the same as he used to taunt me by holding my precious potted seedlings over his head, out of my reach just because he knew how important those were to me.

I can't trust anyone but my sisters—least of all *him*. But I need my last connection to my family back even if he's spouting nothing but lies otherwise. "You swear that you'll return the grimoire to me in exchange for my help, regardless of whether or not Lowell's name is cleared? In front of these witnesses? Think before you make an empty promise. We don't take broken vows lightly in this town."

Nolan's gaze holds mine with an intensity that I'm glad he hasn't pinned me with before because it's full of hot promises of violent retribution and sexy celebration times after a victory. "I swear it."

I'm not surprised when he rubs at goosebumps on his arms because the same shivers dance up mine. His words carried weight as though our immortal mothers witnessed the binding vow.

Glancing at Kiva and Dottie, I find the sisters who'll support me no matter what. "Then meet us tonight at the Hack and Ale. We can discuss plans."

It's a date I don't want, but I won't miss it.

5

NOLAN

So much for gaining Sadie's cooperation being the easiest part of this trip. How did a fated-mates connection carry through her human death and into this mortal life as a deity daughter? I thought coming here to face her and bail would be the challenge, but the *real* problem will be staying away from her.

When the mating call started, she was fifteen to my twenty-three. It'd been a no-brainer to keep my distance from the jail bait who could've ruined my career as a rookie. Plus, Lowell wouldn't have forgiven my making a play for his fiancé's under-aged sister—mate or not.

But then, the calling had been weaker, quieter. Now, it screams at me with every curve of her lips, tilt of her head, or hit of loneliness and longing in her gaze. She's looking for some-thing, and part of me wishes that *I* could be that something. My wolf wants to hunt our mate until she claims us. My human side knows better. Tangling with Sadie would be a career killer if not a death wish.

The famous tourist destination they call Syn City's Pleasure District seems deserted, but when I push into the building with *Hack and Ale* spelled out on the unlit neon sign, the place's packed with people crammed into the booths to the left and on stools at the bar ahead. The rattle of glasses and loud laughter are deafening. It smells like beer, burgers, and bad intentions.

Behind the bar, a Black woman built like a linebacker pours drinks. Her braids spill out of a gold bandana that matches her shirt with a snake-haired woman's face printed on the front. The snakes make me shiver, but this woman walked by me earlier while I waited for Bunny outside The Rink, and bartenders know all the gossip. I head her way, not stopping when she scowls at me.

Propping against the bar, I plaster on a friendly smile. "Hi, I'm—"

"The world doesn't revolve around you, marshal. Take your cowboy self somewhere else." She walks away, leaving me with no info, no drink, and no choice but to wait for the Furies. Except every other woman wearing yellow or gold gives me the same cold stare.

I'm used to being shunned as law enforcement, but Syn City has its own rules, and it doesn't take a wise old owl shifter to figure out that I'm not wanted here. Not surprising seeing as how Sadie picked this bar for our meeting.

A cheering crowd fills the narrow doorway to my right. I wander that direction, dodging as many yellow shirts as possible. On the other side of the opening, a wood-paneled room has lanes that end in enormous, scarred bullseye targets along the far side. Sawdust lines the floor. Women with neon-colored hair wearing various shades of blue jump in place as though they're holding pom poms rather than short spears. Their hot pink and electric blue pigtails bop in time to their chant of *hack, hack, hack!*

They cheer encouragements to someone in their midst even as they back away—as though they don't want to risk messing up their pigtails. I don't need to see her to know Sadie's in there. The mating bond shouts that she's in the middle of that crowd.

I peer over the bouncing spears. Sadie meets my gaze and

shoots me a wicked smirk of violent promises. She's gone from a cowardly cutie hiding in her garden to her own kickass brand of chaos, and I can't look away.

I'm gonna need a drink.

With a steady hand, she hurls an axe that hits the center of the bullseye with a loud *whomp*.

Make that a double.

Hack and Ale indeed. Who'd have thought the hack would be literal?

While she was practically Lowell's little sister, it was easier to tell myself to taunt her like a brat and ignore any pesky attraction. But now? The only thing standing in the way of a mating bond is the secret I've hidden my whole life. Plus the fact that she can't stand me.

But what if I could convince her otherwise? What if she could be an ally rather than an obstacle on my way to the rank of a captain? If she has information to help me catch the serial killer, the promotion's guaranteed.

Guilt hits me in the chest as hard as Sadie threw that ax. I couldn't save my brother, couldn't catch his killer, and here I'm thinking of using his fiancé's beloved sister as a pawn in earning my promotion. I blame my beast, the one that's not a wolf, for such devious thoughts.

"I win," she tells a Huntress whose green is outnumbered in a sea of blue fabric with a few purple sequin numbers and Sadie's black.

"You cheated," the Huntress says. "Using a weapon to call isn't allowed. It's a desecration of the immortals' sacred objects."

"Wrong Fury." Sadie unfurls the whip that she had earlier. "Axes and blades have never been my thing, but if you want a demonstration." She lashes it toward what I assumes the other woman's ax stuck in the second ring of the next target. With a loud *snap*, the whip slices through the ax's handle as if it was butter instead of wood. "You owe the Muses a round. A deal's a deal."

The Huntress opens her mouth to protest when a taller, green-wearing woman puts a hand on her shoulder and shakes her head. "You heard the deal. Drinks for the Muses."

Spear-clutching warriors cheer and head for the bar in a wave of blue and neon-colored pigtails, leaving room for me to cross to the targets. I whistle at the precision of Sadie's aim. "Damn, impressive. I didn't know you were a champion ax thrower."

"There's a lot about me you don't know." She loses the spark of anger that she had when proving a point to the Huntress, and I want it back. When she goes to tug her ax free, I don't move away, crowding her to see if I can provoke the temper that makes her eyes flash.

The taller Huntress scowls at me. "Did you adopt a stray?" she asks Sadie.

"Hardly." She banishes the whip, and I want to ask her to recall the thing and do it again. There's no sheathing or holstering for the Furies. Nope, they *poof* their weapons away as though they're storybook wands. I wonder if all the Houses can do it. "Nolan's the wolf marshal sanctioned by our Syndicate to investigate the shifter murders."

"Nolan?" The woman looks down her nose at me despite the fact I have four inches on her. "Sounds like you two are cozy for a Fury who supposedly hates shifters."

"Do you have an actual point, Devlyn?" Sadie asks, sounding tired. "Want me to defy the Syndicate's order to cooperate with the marshals so you can have a legit reason to report me to my coach? Or are you just bitter that your Housemate lost a bet?"

Devlyn. I search my memories for the name and remember her saying the woman was the leader of the Huntresses. Makes sense with the green tunic thing that has music notes, grapes, and what looks like a forest woven in a darker thread. The woman smells wild—like shifter that I can't place, and the scent makes me uneasy. I want to rest my hand on the butt of my gun in case she tries something, but I left it locked in the cabin after the earlier warning. I could almost swear I've scented her before at marshal headquarters. Or maybe someone like her.

Drawing herself up as if she's magically starched into that uppity pose, she says, "We Huntresses honor our promises. Keep a leash on your marshal. Or we will." She sweeps out of the room like a fricking queen, the other Huntress trailing in her wake.

"Wow." I stare after them, wondering if picking a fight with the woman's worth it or if I should simply let the insult go. This isn't a shifter-run town, and I'm already not well liked for whatever reason. Plus, she's packing crazy that I can't quite place. "She's got a hell of an ego."

Sadie snickers. "That's rich coming from you, your royal cockiness." Her grin lights up her face, and I stare until she looks away. "I see you still wear the hat," she says. "I wondered when you showed up without it earlier today."

She remembered.

I touch the brim of my Stetson. It was something Lowell and I shared. Mine has always been black to his brown. We spent our childhoods working the alpha's massive farms—me more than my brother, but that's what comes with being the bastard kid that the alpha needed out of sight, out of the pack's mind. "Some things haven't changed."

"Everything else has," she says.

I hope for both our sakes that she isn't right since the mating call buzzes louder the closer she gets. When she reaches past me to tug the broken handle of the other ax, I lift my hand to help, but she jerks it out of the wooden target as if it's nothing.

"Shifter strength?" I ask.

"Fury strength," she corrects. "Never underestimate the extra strength or speed that the immortals granted their respective Houses."

"What about the Huntresses?"

"If being self-righteous, pretentious nitpickers was a super-power, they'd be the most powerful House in Syn City. As it is, they run this town because they win the roller derby champi-onship." She points, almost jabbing me in the arm with her finger. "Do *not* mention that to Kiva if you don't want her going hatchet happy on you. She already doesn't like you."

"But you do. Or at least you did once."

Her gaze goes sad. "Like I said, things change." She racks one ax while carrying the pieces of the broken one. "Come on, let's get a drink and you can tell me what you have besides an arrowhead to connect the shifter murders to my family's."

"Massacre. That's what your family's house was when I showed up. I'm so sorry, Sadie."

"A little late for apologies. Besides, it wasn't your fault."

Except she's wrong. If only I'd listened when Lowell said someone had followed him to the Tucker house the week before, if I'd called in a patrol to watch the house, if I'd paid attention to the magic-hating trolls spouting off anti-spellcraft rants in the media. *If, if, if.* "It was."

"No, it was mine." With that horrible lie, she walks away, ending the subject and leaving me to follow her or stand there like an idiot while some of the pigtailed blue-shirts—now carrying frothy sweet-smelling glasses of beer—prep to throw their spears at the targets.

This place is an asylum with the insane Houses running the show.

6

SADIE

I LOVE A GOOD AX TOSS TO BURN OFF STRESS. HAVING NOLAN SHOW up when it was my turn to toss and cinch a win against the Huntress? A delicious bonus.

After my ax struck the bullseye, his wolfish gaze had roamed over my face, and it wasn't panic or alarm in his eyes. It was desire —sexy and distracting—along with a look of *challenge accepted*. Not the reaction I'd hoped for. My heart raced in response until he reminded me that he found my family's bodies. Loss pours over me. Three years since the tragedy, and grief leaves me breathless and drowning in a sea of regret when I least expect it.

Pushing through the cheer squad of Nymphs who thank me for winning them free beer, I spot Dottie waving from a small booth and head her way, dodging a couple of Muses toasting each other's awesomeness with champagne. Their drinks slosh, spilling sickly sweet smells into the air and onto the hardwood floor.

Kiva pushes past me. "No room in our booth for you tonight, but the Nymphs saved you and the wolf a cozy table for two."

"You must be joking," I say. She's not. A tiny round table shoved in the corner stands open with a little sign that says *Reserved* in bubble print. All it needs is a flickering candle to suggest a date. *As if.* I'd rather hang out with the sea hags at the swamp's edge. But if I was wrong about Lowell, I could be wrong about an entire species. Doubt has me dropping into one of the two seats.

Nolan takes the chair across from me, stretching his long legs until his boots encroach on my space.

Awkward.

Luckily, Tisia comes striding from behind the bar and slides two full glasses across the scarred table. The one meant for me has a pale golden shine. Nolan's looks darker, more robust.

"Thanks," I say.

"No worries," she tells me. "Just don't forget to show me that makeup trick."

Nolan eyes his beer as if it might bite. "I didn't order anything."

"Don't test me, marshal," Tisia answers before stomping back behind the bar.

"What'd I say wrong?" he asks me in a lower voice.

"You exist. That's enough 'wrong' for her. Gorgons don't like men." I take a sip of mine, letting the honey sweetness coat my tongue. Usually, I'm served a bitter beer. This candy-like brew has a hint of something floral beneath. I'm still trying to place the taste when Nolan leans forward, almost bumping me with that damned cowboy hat of his.

"The bartender looks like she could break me in half," he says.

"She probably can, although in Syn City, you can't judge someone's strength simply based on their looks." I drink again, taking a full gulp this time and wondering what that flowery note might be. It's subtle.

Nolan sniffs his. "Do you think she poisoned mine?"

"With snake venom," I lie. He hated snakes when we were

younger, and given the way he wrinkles his nose, I'd guess he still does.

"Nope. I know the scent of that, and it's not in here. Any other possibilities?"

"Doubtful," I admit. "With your shifter senses, you'd be able to smell any chemicals, and I raise the only poisonous plants in town."

He shoots me a narrow-eyed stare. "Let me guess. You grow wolfsbane?"

One of the few herbs that can kill a wolf shifter. "Of course I do." Why wouldn't I after a wolf shifter murdered my family? Or at least I thought he had.

"Just enough of the non-lethal breed for personal protection, right?"

"That rule only applies in marshal jurisdictions. Not here. Some of my wolf's bane grows waist high, and I have an extra-deadly species that typically only grows on mountain tops in Nepal. Funny thing about the magic in Syn City. It doesn't always work the way you expect, but it yields the richest soil. Want to visit my new garden?"

"Another time," he demurs. "Does the bartender always pick your drink here?"

"She knows which ale you need most."

"What if you don't like it?"

"You will." Tisia never fails. "It's either her magic or something in this bar that allows her to match you with what serves you best at that moment. Be glad Mad Maes don't run the place. The daughters of Bacchus would slip you a psychedelic just to see what you might do."

"Is everything magic in this town?"

"Pretty much," I admit.

Drinking the ale, he glances at me over the rim of his glass. "*Mmm*, it's like licorice, but better," he says. "Mostly bitter, some sweet."

I go through a mental list of the possible plants that could create the taste he described. "Tisia?" I call, raising my voice. "Did you give the marshal a beer made with mugwort?"

The Gorgon flashes a sly smile. "It'll help him swallow any bitter truths."

I'd almost forgotten her mother had been a kitchen witch. "And the honey in mine? That have a purpose?"

"Wouldn't hurt to sweeten you up a bit," she says. "I added the rosehip and lavender just for you. Plus, I poured a little spicy kick with buckeye for your new friend." Damn her, the snake venom might've been safer than an ingredient used in sexy time spells for stamina and virility.

My stomach rolls and I swallow hard to choke down the sip in my mouth. "Very funny."

She laughs. "I thought so." With that, she moves to separate a trio of Nymphs who shake their spears as fast as their hips to whatever song they've convinced the Muses to play over the speakers.

"She put flowers in your beer?" Nolan sounds as if Tisia committed treason.

"Yep." No way will I tell him that she laced my drink with ingredients commonly used in love and attraction spells. The joke's on her. It won't work on me. I don't think. Hmm, maybe I shouldn't have chugged half of it.

"Your pep squad with the neon pigtails," he says in a molasses-slow drawl. "Who were they?"

"Why? You have enough of an ego that you don't need a cheerleading team." He always had confidence, and I'd thought it sexy until he turned it against me. "Unless you're looking to get laid."

"They aren't my type."

"The Nymphs are literally *everyone's* type." I really need to slow to tiny sips of this ale, but it's so smooth.

"I don't want to have to babysit a date to make sure she

wouldn't stab herself with a spear. Those women ever been shown how to hold those things safely?"

"Nymphs are lovers, not fighters. Stone does the best he can to teach them how to use the weapons he makes, but if their favorite song comes on, forget about it. They'd rather dance and swing the spears around than worry about which end's pointy."

"Who's Stone?" he asks.

"Kiva's bear shifter mate. He's the local blacksmith, and he teaches a training school for combat techniques."

"I think his school's outside the cabin I'm staying in."

I don't want to think of where he's staying, where he'll be sleeping off Tisia's brews tonight. "Two murderers have terrorized our town, and the serial killer you're hunting has hit two shifter packs within fifty miles. Even the Nymphs need to know how to defend themselves. At least Kiva talked them into going with spears instead of the maces they originally requested."

The mild horror in his gaze makes my sharing worth it. Good, it's time I took control of this conversation. "About your investigation—"

"The head Huntress," he interrupts. "Devlyn. She seems familiar." He makes it sound as though I should know where he might have seen her before.

"I don't know, marshal." I put a strong emphasis on his title. "You're the detective. You figure it out."

"You sure you didn't know her from..." His hesitation draws out far longer than comfortable.

"From before I died?" I shoot him a *yeah I said it* look. "No, I never met the woman before I became a Fury. Wouldn't matter if I did since a lot of the Houses undergo a physical transformation at their turns."

"You didn't."

"Furies die. That's transformation enough."

He doesn't flinch at the snap in my tone that lashes like my weapon to call. "I swear I've scented her before."

"Gross."

"Shifters rely on scent the same other species rely on sight or sound. If I could just place the memory." Turning his glass in a slow circle, he stares at the beads of water along the side as if the answer might be there. "I wonder when she might've been at marshal headquarters."

"Uh, never. Huntresses think shifters rank as pets at best."

"Still, I know that scent."

I don't have time for him to sift through his memories of whatever women he has met, dated, banged, whatever. "What makes you think the shifter murders are related to my family—"

He interrupts again, staring at me. "Your wings—they look like your family's grimoire."

"You only know that since you stole it." Rage crawls through my veins, inciting the familiar wish for revenge. "Why do you think my murder's connected to a serial killer?"

"What happened to your wings?"

"What happened to you answering my question?" I try for bitterness in my tone but fail. What else did Tisia put in my drink?

Nolan keeps that calm cop face.

I want to provoke a response, maybe more of the heat and hunger I saw in his gaze earlier. Instead of indulging in that insanity, I glance around the other tables, taking in the clink of glasses and thudding of weapons hitting their targets in the Hack Alley. "When I want my wings, they're there. When I don't, they're gone."

"No, I'm talking about the symbols that flicker across them. They look...wrong somehow."

Tisia sets another two ales in front of us and clears our empty glasses. When the hell did I finish mine? I don't even remember.

I keep my gaze on her, the table, the bar, anywhere but him. "A Fury's wings tell part of how her first life ended. Like I said, the magic in Syn City sometimes warps things from what you'd expect." I don't mention the messed-up sigils are proof of how I failed my family. "Anything else you need to know before we discuss the reason you're here?"

When I look his way, he's staring at me. His focus is intense and unnerving. I struggle to keep my mouth shut and my thoughts on the conversation.

"Whoever is committing the shifter murders—and I haven't ruled out the possibility of multiple killers—they target victims who matter to their community."

I hold up a finger. "Everyone matters."

"Agreed, but the loss of some victims have a greater impact than others. Kill an outcast or a criminal? Shifters protest less. Murder the child of an alpha or brutally attack any kid, and the pack's dealt a crippling blow."

"You're talking about the teenaged girl from the bear shifters and Lowell from your family's pack." I need to make sure I'm following his logic and not assuming anything.

"Yes. Them and every other victim. Each was a targeted strike at the shifter communities around them."

"Okay, but how is that relevant to my family's murder?"

"Your sister was Lowell's mate; therefore, her home was under the pack's protection. Your father was on the city's human board of supervisors—the only practicing spell-worker. Your mother was a pivotal member of the interspecies council."

"So my baby sister and I were what? Collateral damage?"

He hesitates. "Witnesses who couldn't be left alive. Do you remember *anything* about your killer that would help the investigation?"

"I had my back to the front door, running upstairs for the grimoire to find a protection spell. I never saw whoever killed me. I only heard my family screaming. I thought I could save them."

"You tried."

"I failed," I whisper, almost forgetting that even in a deafening bar, his shifter senses would let him hear me.

"Not your fault."

"Maybe I'll believe that someday." But not today.

He goes silent for a long moment, not filling the space with unwanted reassurances. "Can you talk me through the alliances here, the staff, any locals you know from the communities around Syn City? Who might have a reason to hate shifters?"

I narrow my eyes. "Other than me?"

He doesn't take the bait I dangled so easily in front of him. "There has to be some old rivalry or tension here that would explain motive, but I can't even keep the Houses straight."

"That I can help you with." Grabbing my drink, I push to a stand. "Come on."

"Where are we going?" He unfolds his lanky frame like it'll take him all day to stretch to his full height. Every woman's gaze in the bar turns to watch him.

A flush runs over my skin at the unwanted attention. Seriously, that's the *only* reason. It has nothing to do with his sexy self. "The Gorgons put labeled House photos in the bar's back hallway for the tourists." Plus, taking him back there to gawk at pictures will get me out of the sudden spotlight with everyone's eyes on us.

He ambles behind me, his boots making a slow, steady thump. Add some spurs and the man could star in the old Western movies that my parents used to watch together, snuggling on the couch. *Stop.* I can't let the past muddle my head, can't give in to grief. Not for anything. Certainly not with the cowboy cop following me, probably ready to swoop in on any weakness I might show.

I wrap anger around me like a security blanket, but it chafes instead of comforts. "Aside from your victim profile and the arrowheads, how do you link my death to the murdered shifters?"

"The brutality and manner of the kills."

"Yeah, I got that. What else?"

He doesn't offer any further explanation for why he wants to make me relive my worst trauma. Moseying along the hallway, studying each framed photo, he acts as if I'm not there. I'm ready to crawl out of my skin and demand answers when he taps the photo of Devlyn and her team. "You sure the arrowhead couldn't have come from the Huntresses?"

"You heard Kiva. She asked Devlyn and she said the arrowheads didn't come from them."

"What if the Huntress lied?" He cuts a side eye my way, a fierce look that has my insides heating. Damn Tisia for putting love potion ingredients in my drink. "To protect herself or her House, she could've, right? I mean they obviously don't like wolves."

I clear my throat, concentrating on his question instead of how he moves closer. "No, the Huntresses are a lot of terrible things, but they have an impeccable reputation for honesty. They're open with their awful."

He makes that same non-committal noise. "If someone here in Syn City *is* the killer I'm chasing, you're in danger as the one person who might be able identify them."

"*If* the shifter murders are connected to my family's—and I'm still not convinced of that—then like I told you, I didn't see anything."

The dreadful warning in his gaze sends a chill through me. "But the killer or killers don't know that."

"You can't scare me."

"You sure about that?" He trails his fingers along my bare arm, skimming in the lightest touch, and my breath stills in my chest. "Neither of us can handle what my wolf wants from you. It terrifies me."

"Bring your worst." My fighting instinct screams to bat his hand away, to yell at him to get the hell out of my space and out of my town, but I can't move. No, instead of listening to logic, I freeze and stare as his gaze goes amber instead of warm brown. My heart races, but otherwise, I'm motionless.

"Oh, I'll bring my very best." Nolan leans closer, his wolf eyes locking on my mouth before flaring golden. "Final chance to fly away, little Fury."

"I don't run." The rest of whatever I'd meant to say about cowardly wolves and fairy tales and grandma's house dries on my tongue. He scents the air as if I'm prey, and it makes me shiver for all the wrong reasons.

"Good to know." His grip tightens on my arm, hauling me against him. Then his mouth crashes down on mine. He presses me against the wall in a hungry, deep, all-consuming kiss that tastes of beer and man. The growl in his throat has me wanting to crawl up him, around him, inside him. I can't get enough of Nolan freakin' Bankston.

I'm so screwed.

7

NOLAN

KISSING SADIE BURNS ME FROM THE INSIDE OUT. I CAN'T SLOW THE need that has me pushing her against the wall, ready to take anything and everything she'll offer. She tastes of honey sweetness and angry heat. When she slips her tongue against mine, the woman's rage and craving rolls into unyielding demand. I'll give more, more, more until we both drown in desire.

She moans into my mouth, and my wolf wants to devour the sound. All the air rushes out of my lungs. My world tilts and fixes on Sadie as its center. Vivid colors unwind from her in a sea of muted grays.

The mating call howls within me—a bright and shining hope that hauls me out of the darkness and hurt that has haunted me for three long years. I need Sadie to claim me, to accept me, to want *me*. No matter what lies I might have to tell her.

I'm lost in her, and I've no wish to be found.

In my jeans pocket, my phone rings and buzzes like a bomb set to go off. She whimpers, moving away enough to allow a sliver of cold between our bodies.

"Not answering it." I bite the words out against her, barely leashing my wolf's eagerness to nip her kiss-swollen mouth. Her lower lip catches against my teeth, and I want to take with a savage need that hurts deep within. No one's important enough to interrupt this. Not when I feel as though I've been thirsty forever and finally found the one mate who could quench that longing.

Pulling her against me, I hike her leg over my hip and rub against her, marking her with my scent and driving myself insane in the process. Beneath my hands, she's soft curves and long lines. I inhale her, and she smells of earth and herbs, of sage and Sadie. Her warm breath mixes with mine, making my nerves crackle with each gasp, every sigh.

The damn phone rings again, obnoxious and unending. "Ignore it," I command with the alpha power I pretend I don't possess.

"Well, you won't ignore me." A bossy female voice behind me has me spinning. I don't know the woman with dark skin and dreads, but I'm guessing that Sadie does from the way she jumps away from me. I need to add supernatural speed to my mental tally of her newly acquired skills. The newcomer gives us both a hard stare.

"Maizie." Sadie swipes at her mouth as though she can wipe away all traces of our kiss. My wolf doesn't like it. Hell, *I* don't like it. "Coach," she adds quickly, and the respect in the title has my stomach twisting and my spine stiffening.

The woman wears all black and carries herself as if she's in charge. She must be the leader of the House of Furies. I hadn't planned on meeting her, and if I had, it wouldn't have been like this. Clearing my throat, I go for charming and respectful, tipping my hat in her direction. "Ma'am."

She doesn't look amused. No, she looks ticked off. "I'm guessing you must be the wolf marshal."

Yep, she's definitely angry, but I can't lie to the woman when there's a star-shaped badge hooked on my belt. I drop the ma'am in case that might've been what irritated her, especially since she looks younger than me and doesn't sound Southern. Pretending I'm testifying under cross-examination in a court, I settle on giving her the minimum amount of information. "I am."

"What are you doing in the back hall of a bar with one of my Fury's lipstick smeared across your face?" she asks.

"Uh." I don't know how to play this when she walked in on us up against the wall going at each other like we'd lose our minds if we couldn't touch each other.

Maizie or Coach or whatever she wants to be called—just not ma'am—doesn't allow me time to think through a smartass answer. "You came here to investigate murders, correct?"

"I did." Damn, the woman could give my captain a run for the *most patronizing boss of the year* award.

"Did you find your answers somewhere down Sadie's throat? Because if not, I would suggest you look elsewhere and fast. After you put a stop to the killings, then you can fool around all you want *outside* my city. Her past makes her vulnerable, and I won't let you use your so-called shifter authority to take advantage."

Sadie scowls. I'm guessing she doesn't like someone suggesting she's fragile or weak. Especially not when it's the equivalent of her commanding officer doing it. "Coach," she says, the pissy in her voice the same level of *take no crap* she used on me earlier. "It wasn't like that. It didn't mean anything."

Keeping my mouth shut despite the bitter comebacks flooding my brain, I stare at the woman that my wolf insists is our mate, waiting to hear her explain away our kiss.

Her coach lifts a hand. "I don't care what it meant. The Syndicate handed down a ruling tonight. With the ban on tourism and the shifter murders coming closer and closer to our town, they've given the marshal two weeks to solve his case."

Sadie flicks her gaze to me. "Or else he leaves?" The hope in her voice doesn't bother me, or at least that's what I tell myself.

"Or else they shut down The Rink," Maizie says. "No more

roller derby, concerts, or events. With all that gone, soon there will be no more Houses."

"They can't." Sadie sounds horrified.

"Sure they can," the woman answers. "You should also know that the Huntresses will have first rights to the land. Since they won the last derby cup, they'll be crowned the eternal champions. That title comes with power. They've proposed to turn Syn City into a destination hunting preserve."

I interrupt. "What's that?"

The woman glares at me. "A place where rich people pay to come into what's left of the town so they can shoot animals trapped here either by the swamp or fencing."

Sadie's arguing now like she can change the Syndicate's mind if she yells loud enough they can hear her in whatever lair they hide in. The idea of shutting down what's been a huge entertainment town for decades to play trap-the-kill for some rich humans? It sickens me yet it's not technically my problem so I keep my mouth shut.

Pulling my phone from my pocket, I glance at the screen. Below the missed calls, there's a text from Captain Zaleski. *Solve this case in the next two weeks or else the upper brass says turn in your badge.*

Well, shit. That can't happen. If they fire me, I'll lose more than just a job. To have any shot at proving Lowell's innocence, I must remain with the marshals, and I need Sadie's cooperation. *Now.*

I cut into their argument when Sadie stops talking long enough to take a breath. "We'll solve the case and meet their deadline."

Maizie studies me as though she can sense a lie. Maybe she can. "Good," she says. "See that you do." With that, she turns around and leaves me alone in the hallway with one furious Fury.

Pissed-off Sadie Tucker is a marvel of terrifying beauty with flushed cheeks, kiss-smeared lipstick, and blonde strands mussed from that tight ponytail. She also looks ready to use me for target practice which makes me glad that she left that big ass ax over in the hurling gallery.

Poking her finger into my chest, she whispers in an almost hiss, "Would it be too much to expect you to dial down your ego for a minute to consider what you just promised? You marshals have investigated these killings for years. Not weeks, *years*. More shifters die every few months, and I don't hear you revealing any leads except wanting to rehash my family's tragedy. While you may not have a stake in keeping the Houses going in Syn City, I sure as hell do."

"I have plenty of stakes in this game."

She gets in my face. "It's not a game. I *died*. Whoever's killing those shifters? They killed Kiva. We're talking about people's lives."

"I know." I can't keep the edge out of my voice. "They ripped Lowell into pieces the same as they did your family. My brother was the only one to accept me unconditionally since I was a... " The word *kit* almost falls out of my mouth because my first shift as a kid was how the wolf alpha learned that I wasn't his son. No, I belonged to the fox alpha who had an affair with my mother, who came from a line as close to royalty as wolves could have. "A pup," I manage to add without too much of a pause.

Sadie stills, something akin to sadness sliding across her expression before the spark of rage fills it again. "My helping you with the investigation might not prove that Lowell didn't kill me."

"You don't know the whole truth."

"Neither do you."

I want to argue but that won't help win her cooperation. No, I need to de-escalate this situation fast if I have any chance of finding out what she knows or getting my mouth back on hers for another kiss. One that'll prove she lied when she said our first didn't mean anything. Not the way her heart's still racing and my blood's pumping. I raise my hands in mock surrender. "Why don't we get something to eat and discuss strategy?"

"Oh no." She recoils as though I've suggested we have sex with an audience of the Nymphs, grumpy Gorgon, and whoever else we left back in the bar. Not that I'd be opposed, but I'd like my dick to stay attached, thank you very much, and she looks like she might be planning to remove it. She jabs my arm again with her pointy, polished fingernail. "I am *not* falling for the *feed a girl and start the mating dance* routine. Not for you or any other shifter."

"Whoa, who said anything about mates?" *Me*, my wolf chimes in. He can shut the hell up. No matter that the mating bond has me seeing blood red in ribbons around her as though her anger has come to life.

"You *kissed* me."

"And you kissed me back." Okay, I admit, not the smartest comeback. Being with this woman zaps my brain. I swear she sends my thoughts spinning like a tornado coming through hill country.

"Because of the beer Tisia served. Mine had love potion ingredients, and yours came hopped up on virility. The hormone rush? Just a side effect of good kitchen witchery. This wasn't a crazy fated mates thing. I don't want you to feed me or bring me gifts or act in any way that wolves do for women they like. Not now, not ever. Clear?"

"Got it."

"Good." She blows out a breath that has the loose strands of her hair flying, and my fingers itch to smooth it, but I don't move. Not when she looks as though she's about to heft a boulder of worry and I might be the first to get squashed. "What can you tell me that I don't already know about my murder?"

I don't rise to the challenge in her go-screw-yourself-sideways tone. "All right, princess." *Who will always be too good for me.* She bristles at the nickname, and I make a mental note to use it often.

"If Lowell murdered your sister, you, and your entire family before killing himself, how did Hazel's engagement ring go missing?"

"Because someone from the marshals stole it before the coroner's office showed up to take the bodies."

"I arrived first on scene."

Her cheeks go pale, and she curls her hands into fists before nodding. "You said that already. Go on."

"Whoever killed them? They took your sister's ring with them which proves Lowell didn't do it." I drop the verbal bomb and wait for the emotional explosion. Three-two-one, *boom.*

8

SADIE

My garden's my refuge. Sinking my fingers into the damp earth to work new seeds into the soil, I breathe in the sweet herb scent. There's no weeding to bother with—the joy of deity level magic in this town.

A *swish* across the clearing has me looking up. Dottie and her butterfly wings flutter above the lavender blossoms.

"Your garden's so pretty," she says.

"Thanks." I brush my hair out of my eyes. The way Dottie expertly hovers, it's hard to remember my Fury sister couldn't fly that long ago without crashing into trees. "Did Coach send you to talk to me?" It's late afternoon, and I've been out here for hours. After finding me kissing Nolan last night, I honestly didn't think it would take this long for someone to come looking for me.

"Nope. Why? Should she have?" Dottie flaps her big pretty wings and lands on one of the stone lines I've created. The garden forms a wheel—each of the eight sections dedicated to a different poison at the center with herbs beyond and rows of wolf's bane forming the outer ring. "I can stand here, right?"

I treat my garden like a temple. Certain parts can be stepped on, but most can't. My sisters respect the boundaries. "You're safe there."

"You hiding from Coach?" she asks.

"I'm hiding from everyone."

She moves closer. "Well, now I'm not leaving until you tell me why. Does it have something to do with how fast you left the Hack and Ale last night? Or how pitiful the wolf marshal looked after watching you go?"

I fight the urge to ask her about Nolan or shifters in general, especially not the mating part. Except I need to know her take on whether Lowell could've hurt my sister. Dottie and Kiva have both hinted that one mate couldn't physically hurt the other, at least not intentionally. They both seemed shocked that a wolf would've attacked his human. "Nolan said that my sister's engagement ring was gone by the time he came to our house. So either he's lying, someone stole it after the murder, or—"

"The killer took it."

I wish I had a fraction of her certainty. "What if Nolan is lying?"

"Why would he do that?"

"To clear his family's name. To get me to do his work for him since he has two weeks to crack a case he hasn't solved in years. To make himself look good by using my family's murder to build up his reputation in the marshal's office."

"According to Stone's sort-of alpha, Nolan's already the shit in the marshal's office—some kind of golden boy. Kiva said they talked today, and other than some recent mess where Nolan shot a human to save a tortured kid, your wolf has been their top detective for years. They made him the lead on the shifter serial killer case a month ago because he's the best shot at solving it, *not* because of your family's tragedy. Apparently, that was a strike against him seeing as how his brother took the blame."

"So why come here?" So he's competent, well-liked, and a big deal among shifters? I still don't trust him not to have an ulterior motive.

"The reason could be exactly what he said about investigating the two local murders. Not many places around here can house a marshal with the electricity and tech outages that go on in normal towns. We have the best resources, and the Syndicate bent the rules to allow him here. The quicker he stops the murders, the faster they can reopen Syn City."

"You mean Nolan's visit isn't about me."

"I didn't say that. Just maybe that it's not *all* about you." She shoots me a sly smile that has my nerves pinging. Does she know about the kiss?

"What's that supposed to mean?"

"Oh, come on, Sadie. He looks at you like he's going to set the world on fire if he can't touch you."

"Nolan? He spent years either ignoring or antagonizing me. The man can't stand me."

"How long did you know each other before?" *Before your death.* She doesn't have to say it.

"Over a decade. Almost half my first life."

She leans closer to the lavender, letting the stalks brush against her as they blow in the breeze. "Did he always treat you the same?"

"No. He acted like the big brother I never had until my fifteenth birthday. Lugging heavy bags of soil to my garden, pushing me around in the wheelbarrow, bringing me seedlings he thought I might like. Then everything changed."

"On your birthday?" She emphasizes the last word.

"Yeah. I have no idea what I did to make him mad that day, but it was like blowing out the candles on my cake snapped something in him. He couldn't stand me. Why?"

"Fifteen, huh? Sounds about the earliest age that a shifter female can sense the mating call."

I state the obvious. "I'm not a shifter."

"No, but he is. He could've gone from having to act like a big brother to prospective lover in a day."

"Are you saying Nolan was mean to me because he *likes* me?" I don't hide my disbelief. Dottie's so stuck on her mountain lion man that she sees crushes and flirtation everywhere.

"You don't have to fly far to get from love to hate." She flutters from one side of the rock path to the other as if proving her point. "How old would he have been when you turned fifteen?"

I do the math in my head. "Twenty-three, I think."

"He wouldn't have been able to say anything then, especially not if your families were close or if his had political ties."

"His brother was engaged to my sister, and his dad was the alpha of Nashville.."

"So his complications ticked both those boxes. Too bad he didn't try to kiss you."

Memory of last night's kiss has my heart pounding, my face flushing, and my brain completely incapable of focusing on anything but the feel of his lips on mine. "Wh-what?" I sputter. "When?"

"Back then, silly." She skips from stone to stone, using her wings to steady herself. Thank the gods she doesn't glance my way. "Or now. It wouldn't depend really if you were fated to be mates. Kiva and I have proven with our men that the connections span over lifetimes."

"Why? How would a stupid kiss prove anything?"

She stares into the trees, her gaze going dreamy and distant. "The colors. When mates kiss, the world goes from black and white to these beautiful, vibrant shades. It's like a rainbow was hiding behind everything all along, only you couldn't see it. But after a true mate's kiss, your perception changes. *You* change." When she catches me staring at her, she huffs a soft laugh. "Sounds crazy, but it's true. Emotions from your mate ripple through your vision like stormy worry grey or candy-apple anger."

A chill runs through me, winding around my spine like a vine and squeezing my heart like a root ball wound too tight. "What's spiky gold? Like Gorgon yellow but jagged and broken?" The colors that spooled out of Nolan to wrap around me in the hallway last night.

"For me, gold's love, though I've never seen it anything but smooth. Why?"

My chest goes tight. *Love*? I can't. He couldn't. *We* couldn't. Not with the past between us and a future of him in Nashville and me bound to Syn City. "I thought I heard Kiva mention it once. I must've been wrong."

She stares at me, narrowing her eyes. "Any other colors she talked about?"

"Nope." I nod toward the pointed yellow petals on the arnica flowers. "She probably just wanted a way to make sure I didn't dose the healing balm I sent home with her and Stone."

Her glance follows my gaze. "Spiky yellow. Poison?"

"Lethal to certain shifters."

"Well, that'd be a good reason for her to ask." She sounds as if she bought my lie. "At least if Nolan kissed you, then you would know why his attitude changed."

"It's more like he's just an asshole." Because I don't want to talk about that kiss even though it's all I can think about this morning. "His brother was at least a sweetheart before he snapped...or didn't." If Nolan's being honest with me now, then the marshals covered up the actual truth years ago. "I don't know what to think anymore."

"Only you can make that decision. He didn't lose his entire family and get forced into this life. You did. Kiva and I will stand by you no matter what you choose." Her vehemence melts the sharp edges from my anxiety.

Damn, at least one thing's still going right despite the chaotic mess that Nolan has made of me since his arrival. "The immortals knew what they were doing when our mothers chose my sisters in this life."

She flies forward as if coming at me for a hug, big tears dripping down her cheeks. "Aww, Sadie, you made me cry."

"Not on the opium poppies," I warn her, throwing up my hands in the universal *whoa* gesture. "They soak up the tears and pass on the sadness in any brews."

"All right." She covers her mouth as if trying to smother her laughter. "No expressing emotions on the plants. Got it. I'm sure the stoic rule has nothing to do with the gardener."

I toss a clump of dirt at her, the soil that doesn't stick to my fingers or under my nails spraying in an arc.

This time she doesn't bother hiding her giggles.

She laughs and flies up through the trees before dashing away almost as fast as she can skate. The woman may be a walking accident waiting to happen, but she's a speed demon on the track. If only roller derby was back in session.

If only Syn City could reopen.

If only I hadn't kissed Nolan. And gotten caught.

Coach has a direct connection to the Syndicate as the leader of our House. The ruling board doesn't mess around once they've handed down a decision. My stomach churns with the idea of the Huntresses turning our home into some kind of shooting gallery for sport. But it'll happen if Nolan doesn't solve his case.

The case that I can't help with because I don't remember anything about my murder. Which is why I'm hiding in my garden.

I failed to protect my family, can't seek a Fury's revenge, and don't know how to make the current problem go away. So I plant and water, call on the earth to nurture these seeds into sprouts, and switch the order of the stones to best encourage deep roots and lush growth. I work until long shadows stretch across the wolf's bane borders, no closer to answers of what to do about Nolan than when I started.

"Hope I'm not disturbing you." Nolan's voice—rich and smooth with a depth and weight I don't remember—has me flinching. He stands at the edge of the woods, leaning against a tree as if he's been there a while. "I used to imagine you in a garden like this."

Suspicion spirals through me, making me wish I couldn't see ribbons the grey-green of storm clouds unraveling from him. *Worry*, Dottie had said that color represented. What could have a cocky wolf marshal worried? Worse, why does his being bothered trouble me so much?

"How'd you find me?" I ask. "This spot's warded with cloaking spells and protective magic so thick that no one outside my sisters can pinpoint it."

He lifts his chin skyward. "I followed the butterfly Fury."

Dottie. That makes sense. If he could see her above the tree-tops, he must've tracked the most likely location from there. Except the spells should have confused him when he came closer.

"I brought you something," he says.

"Thought I was clear about no mating gifts." I brush my hands against my black apron that has little skulls embroidered on it, a present from Kiva who says I shouldn't have to sacrifice my famous style for the sake of some dirt. "No food, no nothing."

He comes out of the trees carrying a metal box that looks like a friggin' safe. Hell, knowing his shifter strength? It might *be* a safe. Steering clear of the wolf's bane, he puts it on the ground and opens it to lift a cedar chest carved with sigils from inside.

My heart leaps to my throat, and my wings shoot out from my shoulder blades to carry me to him in seconds. "Is that...?" I don't dare hope. The last time I saw that chest was in my family's attic next to the altar.

"Your family's grimoire."

He brought it. *It's here.*

Relief, happiness, and an overwhelming fear launch a war in

my belly. My breaths come too fast, and my eyes burn. I don't know if I want to throw open the lid or tell him to put it back in that damn safe. But he's given me the chance to decide. Before I can let good sense get in the way of staggering sensibilities, I grab him by his scruffy cheeks and kiss him.

9

NOLAN

SADIE'S LIPS ON MINE BRAND ME AS IF SHE'S TWISTING THE MATING call's knife deeper into my chest. Her simple peck of a kiss lights me up like an inferno rages through me, and then she licks the tip of her tongue against my mouth. I almost drop the box with her family's grimoire inside to wrap my arms around her, but she pulls away, leaving me standing there like a starstruck dummy.

Gods, she's so pretty with a little streak of dirt across perfect skin that doesn't need the makeup she sells. She bites her bottom lip, and I swear she does it on purpose to make me want to grab her for another kiss while she flies just out of reach.

"What was that for?" I ask, my voice rumbling over the sudden gravel in my throat.

"A thank you for bringing the grimoire back to me." Those gorgeous wings of hers rustle as she floats eye-level to me.

"That's a hell of a thanks. Tell me what else I can bring to earn another."

She flies back another few feet, but the corners of her mouth curve upward. "I think we've had more than enough kissing."

"Nah, can't happen. So a thanks will get me one? Anything else?"

She glances at the box as I ease it onto a nearby flat stone, wiping dirt away first. "I don't know. You seemed worried."

How the hell did she know I stressed over her reaction to returning her family's grimoire? Unless... "You haven't been seeing anything odd today, have you?"

"Other than you showing up in my garden?"

I don't rise to the challenge in her tone. "Like strange colors?" The same as I can't stop seeing since I kissed her last night and opened the mating call as wide as a barn door on a hot summer day. The same as I followed here to a friggin' spelled secret garden. Thank the gods I saw her butterfly-winged sister shoot into the sky earlier, or I wouldn't have had the plausible deniability.

"What kind of colors?" She eyes me as if I'm talking crazy. Good, it'll keep her from asking questions about how I got past her protection wards.

"The kind that look like auras around people?" *Specifically around me.*

"And here I thought I was the witchier of the two of us."

My heart falls. I'd hoped she felt something for me, but if she's not seeing the signs, maybe I'm wrong. Or she's stubborn and needs more kisses to push the mating bond through that hard head of hers. Or she's lying. With Sadie from before her murder, I wouldn't have suspected that. Now? I'm not so sure. She isn't the same gullible, shy girl. Instead, she's the brave woman who flies up to me and lays a kiss on me.

"Why'd you bring the grimoire to me?" she asks, tracing her fingers over the symbols carved on the wooden box.

"It's yours."

"That's not the deal you wanted to make yesterday."

"I was wrong."

She stops and stares. "Say that again."

"Nope. I'm not falling for that. I admitted it once. That's all you'll get from me."

"More than I believed was possible." There's that taunting, almost playful tone from her again.

"Sadie Tucker, are you flirting with me?"

"If you have to ask, then you haven't been practicing the last three years."

The thought of her *practicing* has me almost growling. My jaw ticks and I fight to unclench it. It's best that I focus on her grimoire and not the sudden jealousy I have no right to feel. "You want me to help you get that to the House of Furies?"

"Can your wolf sprout wings and fly? That's the only way you'd get into our House, and that's *if* you make it past our defenses. We don't let shifters near the House other than mates."

Other than mates. Someday she'll invite me there, and I'll have to figure out a way to sweet-talk a Fury into leaving Syn City. That should be easy enough if I can ever trust her with my secret. *Shit.* This mating dance is complicated. Why can't we just go back to the nearly impossible task of capturing a serial killer that seemed so simple next to this? How did Lowell ever survive getting Hazel to say *yes*?

He didn't.

The thought sobers me, long enough that I notice Sadie hasn't looked inside to make sure I'm not a liar who pretended to return her grimoire. Would serve me right after being a dick about it yesterday. "You okay?" I ask her. "Need some privacy?" Of course she would. She's grieving her whole damn family, and I'm still the asshole.

"More like I need some courage."

"That is one thing you've never lacked. You might not have said much back then, but you were too fearless for your own good."

"Was not."

"Remember that summer you spent in a cast because you fell out of a tree?"

"I was healing it back to health," she says. "The poor thing got struck by lightning. It gave us acorns every year to use in spell work. I couldn't let it die."

"You climbed nearly forty feet up. Could've broken your neck."

"Saved it though." The pride in her voice has me grinning.

"Yeah you did." That damn tree had been taller than the house the last time I was there. My grin falls. At the murder scene. Terrified I would find my mate's body. "What're you scared of, Sadie? There's nothing in there that you haven't already seen."

She won't meet my gaze. "Running to the grimoire is the last memory I have from that life. Knowing I didn't make it in time to save them is my first memory from this one. What if I don't deserve having it back?" Her question comes out on a whisper I can barely make out even with my shifter hearing.

"You did everything you could to protect your family. I don't know how you made it up those stairs bleeding out the way you were." The memory of her blood dripping down the stairs, smeared on the door, puddled on the attic floor, sprayed across the walls—it makes me sick.

"I didn't..." She can't seem to finish her thought.

"They cut you down where you stood. You had no chance. I wouldn't be surprised if you didn't fight back. Isn't that who the Furies pick to turn? Warriors set on vengeance?" I might've investigated more than shifter victims today. The local townspeople love to gossip about their deity daughter neighbors.

She shakes her head. "I don't remember bleeding. It must've been the killer's blood."

"It was yours. It smelled like you."

"No, it couldn't have been mine. I ran—" Panic buzzes green around her in a way that sends mirroring fear through me and has my wolf raising his hackles. We can't stand to see our mate frightened. She might talk tough, but when it comes to strong emotions, the mating bond doesn't lie.

"Sadie, I would know your scent anywhere. That was your

blood, same as it's yours spotting the pages of the grimoire." I tormented myself looking at those stains for hours knowing that she'd suffered.

"Show me." The green pulsing around her fades the slightest.

"All right." I would do whatever she asked to soothe that fear. Moving beside her, I risk a brush of my fingers against the back of her hand. The slight contact soothes the beast inside me. Her skin's so damn soft and warm. "We'll open it together."

Flipping the latch on the wooden box, I lift the top, gently resting it against the hinges. The thing's handcrafted and seems sturdy yet I've treated it as though it's fragile since the moment I hustled it out of the Tucker house.

"See," I say. "Nothing scary except memories."

She looks inside. "You rescued my sisters' books of shadows?" Her hands stroke the two small notebooks, one spiral and decorated with glittery stickers.

"I rescued whatever I could grab before the authorities got there."

"Why?"

"The marshals would've tossed everything or locked it in an evidence box never to see daylight again. The humans might've destroyed it."

She touches a torn sticker of a cat. "They would've burned everything. While they wanted Momma's healing, Daddy's food, and my plants, they didn't want to talk about the spells and love that went into them. The police wouldn't have seen a little girl's drawings. They would've seen magic sympathizers." She turns that searching gaze on me. "That still doesn't explain why you saved it all."

"I couldn't watch someone toss what belonged to you."

"Why not?" She won't let this go. *Fuck.* I need her to quit asking questions. "There was no one left to miss those things."

"I knew you were out there somewhere."

"And you hadn't cared much for my feelings since my

fifteenth birthday. You didn't track me here to Syn City. So why bother taking the grimoire?"

I can't tell her that I walked into her birthday party only to have the mating bond slam into me like a fucking bulldozer, that I couldn't face coming here only to know that the link between us had been severed with her death. Or I'd assumed it had been. "It's complicated."

"Uncomplicate it."

"I can't." If I give Sadie an inch, she won't settle for a mile. No, she'll take my whole world because she doesn't do things half way.

"Hmm." She looks away, picking up the grimoire.

What the hell does that little sound mean? *Hmm*—she knows that she tangles me up in knots and enjoys torturing me? *Hmm*— she doesn't care what I think and only asked to fuck with me? Or *hmm*—she's already forgotten I'm standing here? The way she opens the grimoire and slowly flips pages, it's likely the latter.

"You're sure these blood stains are mine?" she asks.

"Yeah. The book holds your family's scents, or it did until they faded. But the blood smelled like yours."

"If I fought, if it wasn't Lowell who murdered me, how sure are you that you can find my family's killer before the deadline?"

"I've solved every case except this one."

"And the shifter murders," she says.

"Same killer. Solve one and I've closed both. I'm sure of it. Why? You willing to help?" *Please let her say yes.*

"Depends." She hugs the grimoire tighter. "You willing to make me a promise if I say yes?"

"Depends," I echo her answer. "You wanting to go back to Nashville with me and be recognized and applauded for catching the killer? I'd agree to that." The idea of having her close to home makes me more comfortable than it should. Part of me seizes on the fact that she'd be where I would have more time to spend with her, to see her work in her garden, to wish she'd be mine.

Another part just needs her safe and protected. I would hire private security to watch over her every single day.

"I don't want any credit, and I can't leave Syn City."

Her stubbornness kills me. "You didn't choose this place. I know you, Sadie. Or at least you wouldn't have if that horrible day hadn't happened. If you want your old life back, no one would stop you."

"The immortals would. I'm a Fury which means I can't leave Syn City."

"Even if the Syndicate and the Huntresses turn it into a hunting preserve?"

She looks thoughtful. "They'd reassign me to a Fury House in another deity city."

"You can't leave the Furies? Ever?"

"That was the deal when I bargained for another chance at life."

That puts a serious damper on any plans to slowly win her over to the idea of a mating bond. If she can't leave the Furies and I can't leave the marshals...fuck, that means worse than I don't deserve my mate. It means I can *never* have her. "Then what are you asking me for?" Because here I hoped I had made a little headway between the kiss, giving back the grimoire, and then the cozy chat we just had. I couldn't think of anything but her all day which made it damn hard to concentrate on my job at a shifter murder scene.

"Revenge." Her gaze holds fire and sorrow. How the hell can I say no to her after what she and her family suffered? The violence she promises should make her a villain in this terrible mess, but it doesn't. She's not throwing around empty threats or taking out her anger on whoever crosses her path. This is justified execution for crimes committed that I can understand.

"All right. You can have it so long as you don't end up dead again."

"Deal."

This woman with that whip she can call magically into her hand and those wings and her badass beauty—she's fierce, formidable...and hot. I angle closer, hinting that she reward me for agreeing like she did for bringing back her grimoire. She's a heartbeat away.

The *clang* of bells from the Pleasure District have her on full alert, much as a "marshal down" call would have me switching into serious calm before combat. Another echo of bells from the direction of The Rink, and she's shoving the grimoire back into the wooden box and securing the latch. A different shade of red fires off her, bolder than her anger earlier.

"That's the emergency system," she says. "Something's happening. Something big. I need to get to the House of Furies. You okay to find your way to shelter? If not, you can stay here in the wards."

I won't leave her when there's danger. I've already lost her once. "I'm good but—"

She kicks off into the air with the grimoire's chest in her arms. "Nolan," she calls from the treetops, the sky a backdrop of bleeding sunset behind her.

"Yeah?"

"Don't die on me. I'm not done kissing you yet." With that, she's gone.

10

SADIE

I MUST'VE LOST MY MIND TELLING NOLAN BANKSTON THAT I PLAN on kissing him again, but as much as he makes me crazy with his mood swings that go from bribing me with the grimoire to handing my history back to me with no strings attached, I'm not done with my childhood crush. Not yet anyway.

The bells still ring when I land on the House of Furies large wooden porch that serves as our flight deck. Tucking my wings, I hurry inside. Syn City has been terrorized by a serial killer and an evil sea witch in the last few months. Yet today's the first time I've heard those bells ring anything more than a single chime for practice or a few times to signal a game. They've never gone on for minutes.

"Sadie," Maizie yells from inside the House. "Suit up in combat gear. Make it fast. I need you and your sisters with me in the Pleasure District."

"Yes, Coach." I hustle to do as ordered, cradling the chest with my family's grimoire inside until I reach my room where I can leave it in safety.

Growing up, I envied my older sister's talent to make anything beautiful. Her spells tended toward glamor. With a quick twist of hair, fast dab of makeup, or a few well-placed stitches, Hazel could make the ordinary look stunning while remaining practical. I honor her legacy in my cosmetics brand that makes me millions, but my first creation in her memory was designing combat suits for the Furies.

Crafted with top-of-the-line body armor in the most flexible fabric I could find, my suit moves with me when I fight and allows my wings to spread to their fullest. It'll hold everything from a sword to a lipstick, and it looks gorgeous while doing it. In Fury black, the sleek bodysuit has hidden zippers that let me strap into it in seconds.

When I hit the flight deck this time, Furies file out of the House in combat gear. My sisters land near me.

"Nolan was almost back to the cabins when we flew overhead," Dottie says. "He's away from the fighting."

"What fighting?" I ask. Other than the occasional bar brawl, there's no assault and battery in Syn City. All the Houses are too scared of what the other could do in retribution to try it, and there's no one here other than the Houses, staff, and families since we've been in lockdown for weeks. "Did someone finally go stir crazy enough to snap?"

Kiva shakes her head, the silver arrowheads in her wings glistening. "This isn't like anything we've ever seen. There's mass panic in the Pleasure District with deity daughters in a frenzy beating the shit out of each other."

"Furies, move out," Coach yells. "Sadie, on me."

We take to the air in a wave of black vengeance headed toward the hotel, shops, and restaurants that should be nearly empty. I keep pace with Coach and her two triad sisters in the lead as Kiva and Dottie watch my six.

We crest the final trees before the Pleasure District starts. Screams, yells, and crying fill the air from below.

Dozens of deity daughters pour out of the Hack and Ale—Gorgons, Muses, Nymphs, even a couple of Mad Maes. They're all fighting as if they'll tear each other apart. It's a splatter of colors in yellow, purple, blue, and red with blood soaking the ground. Broken glass glistens in the dirt around them.

"Holy Hades," Coach mutters.

"What happened here?" I ask her.

"I intend to find out which is why you're with me." She spins to fly backward, and we circle her as we would at the derby track. "Furies, break up the fighting. Use force as necessary but keep it non-lethal. If you can't defend yourself without killing, abort and let them tear into each other. This is *not* revenge or your deity-ordained purpose."

"What if their crazy is contagious?" someone yells from the back.

"Stay with your sisters. If you see a sister fall into madness, haul her ass out of there and get clear. Now go."

I fight every sisterly instinct I have not to swoop down with Kiva and Dottie. Following Coach, I land a quarter of a mile away from the mob. She joins the leaders of the other Houses.

Standing with the leadership of the seven Houses isn't my thing. I'd rather be alone in my garden or picking out samples for my cosmetics brand any day. The memory of Nolan saying that whoever's killing shifters is targeting their leaders and taking out people who matter? It sends goosebumps racing over my skin. Freakin' paranoia. This is a bar fight gone bad, not a serial killer. Still, I can't banish the thought.

"What do we know?" Maizie asks.

"It's like the whole damn bar went crazy," the leader of the Gorgons answers. "I left for a few minutes to smoke and check on my wife and kid. On my way back from family quarters, I hear this weird-ass yell thundering from inside. I figured it was a shifter showing off." She gestures toward the clash that's being broken up by Furies. "The next thing I know, everyone's fighting and throwing people out the windows, breaking down the door, tossing axes at each other."

"What'd your bartenders put in their drinks?" the Muses' coach asks.

"Same old," the Gorgon says. "A few of the Muses and Nymphs flew off looking scared shitless, but the rest? Well, you see them trying to rip each other to shreds." She glances at the leader of the Mad Maes. "Your House have anything to do with this?" The accusation's veiled, but barely.

"Nope." The leader of the Mad Maes wears red lipstick that I could swear is a shade from my brand. She's in all red from her sparkly headband to her dress to short leather boots. "My maenads and I don't do fighting. We bring a raving madness that's one of dancing, revelry, and orgies."

"Which is why y'all are invited to all our parties," the leader of the Nymphs says with a giggle. These women are our fearless leaders? No wonder we're a roller derby city and not a more conservative or classy venture.

At least Maizie stays on topic. "Could your Mad Maes have accidentally incited a riot instead of drunk sexy times?"

Their leader shakes her head. "We strive for ecstasy, not pain. Unless it's in the pursuit of pleasure. This is panic, not rapture."

"Barbarism," Devlyn announces with full Huntress *superior to thou* snootiness. "You don't see any of my House out there brawling. We save our aggression for roller derby. It's why we win."

"Anything *helpful* to add?" Maizie asks her.

"Ask your poison grower what plants would cause this violence." Devlyn glances my way. "That's why you brought her, isn't it? What else would she be good for other than bedding down with shifters the same as her sisters?"

I step forward, ready to volunteer to show Devlyn exactly what I'm good at which is punching her in her face.

Maizie holds out her hand, stopping me. "Any poison you know of that could cause something like this?"

"No." I keep my hands curled into fists. "I can kill, I can heal, but I can't provoke anything like this. What about the noise she heard? Is there a roar or a noise that could drive people mad?"

"It's a riot," Devlyn says with a sneer. "Not a boxing match with rules and a bell."

A bell. At least the bells have gone silent.

I keep my mouth shut while the Coaches go back and forth with possibilities.

"There's an obvious solution at least for now," Devlyn says. "A temporary stop gap. Keep the poisoner on House arrest. Interrogate the wolf marshal since he's the only new addition to our town plus he wasn't at the Hack and Ale. Destroy the poison garden in case someone else used her plants."

My heart misses a couple of beats, and I can't catch a full breath. "No, you can't. I—"

"Sadie," Maizie says. "Go help your sisters."

"Yes, Coach." I hurt from the inside out, a wound that I can't see but *oh,* I feel it. The garden's been my private sanctuary since I got here, the closest I've come to recreating a piece of my family's home. Still, I do as I'm commanded. It's the Fury way.

Landing near Kiva and Dottie, I check both for injuries. Dottie's ponytail has come undone, but otherwise she looks the same as always. Kiva seems bored with the fighting which makes sense given she grew up battling actual monsters. She forces two Muses apart who seem intent on ripping each other's hair out while Dottie deals with a crying Nymph and a Mad Mae who's rocking back and forth as if she's terrified the big bad wolf's just around the next corner.

Speaking of wolves, at least Nolan's far from here. Maybe Coach will talk Devlyn out of whatever waterboarding or other tortuous interrogation technique the Huntress has in mind for him.

On the outskirts of the mob, I wade into a wrestling pile-on to yank screaming Nymphs off Tisia, tossing them to other Furies to settle. The Gorgon is massive, and this will get bloody quick if she decides to come up swinging. Her braids have come loose, and she has a busted lip, but the Nymphs piled on top of her could've looked much worse than they did.

Tensing in case I need to react, I crouch next to her, holding up my hands. "You all right, Tisia?"

She stares at me, and her wide-eyed compassion breaks my heart. "It didn't get you." The hurt in her voice echoes my pain at possibly losing my garden to Devlyn and her schemes. "Wait, no, you weren't here. The Furies didn't come to Hack and Ale today."

"Most of us had training at the House. I was working on something else."

"This would've been a bloodbath if y'all had been here. I tried to stop it, but I could only do so much against the crowd."

I hold out a hand. She eyes it as if I might have something contagious. "Just wanting to help you away from the fight. My sisters will finish breaking it up. Looks like you could use some first aid." I point to the makeshift medic table some Huntresses are setting up down the way.

Tisia wipes her mouth with a gold bandana from her pocket. "I'm not hurt as badly as some of the others." She takes my hand, and I pull her to her feet. "There's no telling how many broken bones or stitches will come out of this."

"What happened?" When she doesn't answer, I tell her what I know from listening to the coaches. It's not like they swore me to secrecy. "I heard there was a yell, and then all hell broke loose." Which makes no sense. Who has a battle cry that makes people act insane?

She glances at me, then at the chaos left behind as the Furies pull apart the few remaining fighters. "Fear. Paranoia. Absolute panic. Everything was fine until this awful scream came from the back of the bar." Tisia goes quiet and stares at me as if waiting to see if I believe her.

"Could you tell if it was a man or woman?" I don't have Nolan's detective skills, but I can ask basic questions.

"No. I can't even say if it was human. Thank the gods the Furies weren't here, or we'd be carrying everyone out on stretchers with the way y'all are trained in combat."

I help her to a seat on a bench outside the hotel. "Any other Houses not there?"

"The Styx. Those undead ladies don't patronize our bar, and who knows what rattles them given we don't even know what they are."

That explains why the rainbow of House colors in the riot didn't include any Fury black or Styx white. "What about the Huntresses?"

"A couple were showing off their archery skills in the gallery, but the sound didn't seem to bother them."

"I wonder why." It doesn't make sense that they'd be somehow immune.

"Maybe they're so uptight that coming unwound a little just means acting like what the rest of us would consider normal. They kept shooting. The rest of the room, though, lost their collective mind."

"You didn't," I say. Tisia's tough, a formidable opponent on the derby track. She could've taken out a half dozen Nymphs without breaking a gold-painted nail.

"I do a hell of a lot of yoga and meditation to keep my issues under control." She shoots a look at the sobbing Mad Mae and Muse nearby. "A lot of these bitches could use it." Lighting a joint, she takes a long draw and tension seems to ease off her shoulders with the exhale of smoke. "Don't judge. I quit smoking years ago, but I keep an emergency doobie on me in case shit goes sideways. Such as now."

"How'd we get like this?" I can't tell the red of Mad Maes from the blood-soaked baby blues worn by some of the Nymphs. "Going at each other like animals?" Maybe Devlyn has a point. Dear gods, I'm the one whose sanity's slipping if I think *Devlyn* might be right.

"It's not surprising." She takes another puff.

"What do you mean?"

"Deity daughters need a release for the aggression that comes with whatever trauma brought us here. Now, we're all stuck in the city together, House rivalries and tensions running high while rumors run rampant that The Rink's gonna shut down permanently. People with deity daughter powers are not the ones you want going stir crazy and breaking apart when we're locked down. My guess? This is the beginning of an ugly end unless things change."

Devlyn heads our way, a crowd of Huntresses around her. "Tisia, you need to come with us for questioning."

I step in front of the Gorgon. "She's hurt. She needs medical attention, not a lecture from you."

"Make this harder, Fury." Devlyn gives a grin that's anything but friendly. "I dare you."

"She didn't do anything wrong—" I stop when Tisia puts her hand on my shoulder.

"Don't fight them," she says. "It'll just make things worse." She squeezes my arm. "When this is done, we can have that makeup lesson you owe me, all right?"

I can't stand to see them circling her while blood drips from a cut on her face. "But—"

She shakes her head. "I don't need you to rescue me from their stuck-up prejudice. Go find your wolf marshal. Make him solve the shifter murders so this mess can all be over and things can go back to the way they were when you and I arrived in Syn City."

The Huntresses lead her away before I can tell her Nolan isn't mine. But perhaps I can help him fix this before more people get hurt.

11

NOLAN

Winding up in chains wasn't my idea of a good time unless Sadie wanted to test out some kink. Then I might be down to play. But when Huntresses stormed my cabin demanding that I surrender for questioning? Yeah, not how I planned for this investigation to go down. Yet I played along with some high and mighty misses pretending to be cops.

A key jingles in the front door to the hotel. A moment later the scents of bear and rabbit waft my way. At least it's not the mountain lion. Gods, cat shifters annoy me. So damn vain without the pack structure to back up the enormous ego.

"They locked him up in the next room, chained him to the check-in desk," a feminine voice says softly.

"Thanks, Bunny," a much deeper one answers. "You coming with?"

"Nuh uh. He's a predator, trapped and cornered. A wolf marshal at that. I'm no dumb bunny."

"Fair enough."

"Lock up after me, Stone, and remember I was never here."

"Got it."

Footsteps both light and heavy follow, and the door snaps

shut again, a lock clicking into place. The grizzly lumbers my way, the giant's weight making the floorboards creak. He rounds the corner into the room where I'm chained like a dog. "Fine mess you've gotten yourself into here, marshal."

I refuse to show fear. As big as he is, I could take him...maybe. "Might as well call me Nolan seeing as how we're not exactly on formal terms here."

"All right, Nolan. We haven't been introduced all though you've met my wife, Kiva."

"Sadie's sister with the arrowheads for wings?" I don't add her attitude or her big mouth as I'd rather not provoke him into inflicting more damage than he came here to do.

"That's my mate. I'm Stone. Can't say it's good to meet you under these circumstances."

"Did the Huntresses send you?" I don't give him time to answer. "I know Syn City doesn't believe in rights for the accused, but I swear I didn't have anything to do with inciting any riots. Roughing me up won't change that, and I'll fight back. Doesn't matter that you're mated to Sadie's sister or whatever they're called in this life."

He laughs, a rumble that I swear shakes the room. "I'm here despite the Huntresses ordering everyone to stay away from you until they can finish their sad excuse for an investigation. You're not the only one they took."

Fear flares in my gut, hot and ugly. "Sadie?"

"No, wolf for brains, they didn't take her, but I understand they threatened her secret garden that no one but her sisters have ever found."

I don't tell him I found it. "What do you mean threatened it?"

"Kiva says the Huntresses claim her poisons could've contribute to whatever crazy shit happened at the Hack and Ale so they want to destroy the garden."

"No, it'll kill a piece of her." Anger has my wolf rising up as if he can stop them. "They can't—"

"Slow down. Tell me why it matters so much."

He makes the demand seem so calm and rational. I guess it's necessary when dealing with a mate as hotheaded as his. "She had a garden in her first life. It was like having her own kingdom. She can grow anything, heal sick plants and trees, make all kinds of potions and balms to cure aches and illnesses. Her family called her a green witch."

"My mate relies on her salves for roller derby bumps and bruises."

"Some skating injuries are nothing compared to the wounds that Sadie helped heal with her parents' help."

He curves one corner of his mouth into a grin. "You obviously don't know derby. Those bouts are brutal."

Okay, this bear obviously spent too much time in hibernation. I get to the point. "Whoever killed Sadie? They murdered my brother next to her garden and trampled every plant she had, even pulling the ones that weren't crushed out by the roots. It's like they wanted to erase her family's entire existence. If the Huntresses wreck her garden, they'll be forcing her to relive the trauma that's tied to her murder and losing her parents and sisters."

"Aren't you doing that already?" His quiet question slices through me like a million papercuts, painful but not deadly. Not yet anyway.

"I need to catch this serial killer. You know that more than anyone." A cold tactic considering his mate was murdered, yet I'm fine to be that jerk if it means justice gets served.

He comes closer, and I brace for a blow because I probably deserve a punch for poking at that particular wound. I'll let him get a single hit before I start swinging. Only he doesn't curl his hand into a fist. Instead, he reaches into his pocket and pulls out a keyring. Grabbing the chain, he hauls the cuffs on my wrists closer to his face and studies them.

"What're you doing?" I ask when he simply stares long

enough to make me uncomfortable. Not that anything about this situation is remotely comfortable, but I don't need bear shifter breath and massive muscles adding to my problems.

"I designed most of the recent ironworks in this city. Since this isn't silver, I either made it or have made something like it in the past." He doesn't explain further, and he whistles under his breath while he works. It doesn't take me long to decide the grizzly's as irritating as his mate.

I open my mouth to tell him to stop fondling the chains when he pops a key in the lock, jiggles it, pauses, and then wiggles it a different direction. The cuffs open with a clank. "Cool trick."

"The less legal side of blacksmithing. I doubt you'll arrest me for it."

The skin around my wrists burns red and raw, and I rub away the sting. "Won't you get in trouble with the Huntresses?"

He raises one big shoulder. "House rivalries and issues aren't my problem. Come on, Kiva's on the roof as our lookout. We should be clear."

"What if someone spots her?"

"Huntresses can't fly. As for the rest of the Houses, even if they see her, they won't snitch. Besides, Furies are the granddaughters of the night goddess so they blend in scarily well after dark."

I open the mating connection, focusing on the roof. "Sadie isn't with her."

Stone grunts and the sound carries a surprising amount of meaning. "She know she's your mate?"

"What are you talking about…" I cut off the lie at the *don't give me that shit* look from him. "No, she doesn't. Besides, it wouldn't work out between us."

"You're mates. What's there to work out?" He shovels a super-sized dose of sarcasm on the last.

"You wouldn't understand. I'm sure you and Kiva were love at first sight with no issues. You two probably ran away to get married on your second date."

He gestures for me to follow his lead, and I do even though I'm doing so blind because I can't see anything around his giant bear shifter self. "Not that it's your business," he says, "but I'll tell you in hopes that you won't make Sadie's life more difficult. Kiva didn't say yes to marriage until my seventh proposal."

"Man, how'd you fuck it up that many times?" I ask. He stops walking, and I almost crash into him. His low growl sounds like a windstorm coming to knock someone's house down. "All right, all right. Sore subject, I get it."

"My point is that having a mating bond doesn't mean you don't have to work to win your woman." He leads me out of the hotel and into the night, crouched and sneaking through alleyways. A winged shadow darts over us from time to time. "Leave it to a wolf to be lazy about courting."

"Cats are lazy, not wolves." I've worked my human and beast tail off for years to rise in the marshal ranks.

"Chase, the mountain lion shifter mated to Sadie's other sister? He almost died to win Dottie. What would you do?"

Damn, these men are serious about their Fury mates. I decide to break down the obvious for him. "The Furies can't leave Syn City. I'm a marshal, and we aren't welcome here. We can't be a couple."

"Being a marshal's a job. A mate's forever. The choice should be easy."

"Says a guy whose old-timey weapons business was primed for success here in a place where you can't use guns. The marshal's office is the only life I've known." Since Lowell's dad wouldn't openly disown me but made it clear to everyone that I would never be an alpha no matter how much alpha blood I had running through my veins.

"I get you don't want to quit. The shifter murders have to stop. My pack lost a cub. I lost my wife to those psychopaths." His growling returns with the last.

"You suspect multiple killers?"

"And you don't? No one person—unless they're a god or goddess—could do the kind of damage I saw when I found the body of our pack's missing teenager. Whoever killed my Kiva and hacked Rylie into pieces? No shifter would've done that. Rogue or not."

"Unofficially, I agree. The inflicted wounds don't match any known claw pattern."

"Whoever murdered Rylie used knives. Several different blades given the edging and serration of the gouges."

I could use his expertise. The bear's muzzle-deep in this already with his mate being one of the victims, no matter how temporary her death might've been. "Before I got arrested by the Huntresses, I had planned to stop by your school to ask if you and your mate would be willing to help with the investigation."

"Once she finishes guiding us, Kiva will be busy since she and her sisters broke Tisia out earlier."

"Sadie's friend? The Gorgon bartender?"

"Yep. The Huntresses grabbed her first. Claimed she dosed the drinks to make everyone crazy."

"I don't know any spell or drug that could work that kind of magic so quickly on so many people."

"That's what Sadie argued. She's pissed they took Tisia."

But not that they took me. I shouldn't be surprised, but it hurts. "Is that why your mate ran lookout for us and not—" *Mine.* I almost said mine. "Sadie."

The bear scowls at me over his shoulder. "Your mate's been grounded for the night, maybe longer. Huntresses' orders. While the Furies will argue that their rivals don't have the right to physically lock people up, they have to show some cooperation. Sadie said she would play hostage for the night."

I bow up ready for a fight and turn to head back into town.

He stops me with a hand as big as a dinner plate. "Don't worry about her. She turned it into a makeover and television marathon for the Muses and Nymphs who all volunteered to monitor her house arrest. It made for a nice distraction to get Tisia to safety and hide you in my forge."

"Why not the cabin I'm using?"

"Where's the first place they'll look? A cop should know better."

"I'm a cop, not a criminal." Except for tampering with an active crime scene by stealing Sadie's grimoire and her sisters' spell books. "My investigative work's in the cabin. I can't leave it."

"The sealed safe you had in the closet? Or the files hidden under a loose floorboard? Yeah, my woman found those and brought them to the forge for you."

Shit. "That's evidence in an active police investigation."

"Which we didn't poke through. That's more than I can say if the Huntresses had gotten to it first.

True. "I didn't make it easy on them when they came for me. Called it up the marshal chain of command, demanded an audience with their Syndicate, invoked all kinds of legal precedent that I haven't read but wolf lawyers covered in a training. Figured it sounded good."

He grins. "You and Sadie might be a match made in a hell dimension with the way you both frustrate people with your fancy talk until they cave."

"Thanks?"

"You're welcome. Solve the murders. Then you can figure out the mating. We've got a cot and shower at the forge. It's not fancy, but it's better than spending the night in chains. Unless you're into that." He looks back at me. "Not judging if you are." The shadow above us dips lower, and the big man chuckles. "Got to keep things spicy in a marriage."

Great. I might be more uncomfortable now than I was earlier chained to a desk. The rest of the way through the Pleasure District and past the staff quarters, I stay silent and am glad he does the same. The forge stands on the edge of his weaponry school's training grounds. There's a fire pit beside the building along with anvils and other tools I assume he uses.

He nods toward them. "Those are mainly for show. The Nymphs like to pretend to make their own weapons. It usually ends up a pajama party with s'mores."

We push inside where there are more tools along with what looks to be several versions of freakin' Excalibur hanging on the wall beside wicked battle axes. The place smells like smoke and metal.

"Living quarters are in the back," he says. "A beaver shifter built them off the books so the Huntresses shouldn't know. Kiva insists on having multiple places to lay low. Childhood issues. Don't ask."

"I won't, but damn, your mate's life wasn't traumatic enough with murder? It sucks that the Fates added other problems to her mix."

"I got her back in this life so I can't complain too much about what the Fates have in store. That arrowhead you found at Sadie's family home," he says quietly. "You said you've found others like it at the shifter murders?"

"You mean the one that matches your wife's wings?" I still can't imagine how the woman has feathers with silver attached. "All of the arrowheads have been identical except the engravings. We're talking the same killer or killers. Any murderer this reckless and bold with their kills generally wouldn't tolerate a copycat."

He nods and looks away. "I held my wife in my arms as she bled out on a frozen lake only a stone's throw away from the body of the teenager we were out searching for. Young Rylie looked like she'd been slashed to pieces by an angry mob. I crawled inch after inch through their blood."

Shit. I thought *I* had scary memories. "Nothing I can say will help ease that pain except to tell you I'm doing everything I can to solve this case."

"Whoever dumped Rylie's body on that ice? They flew her in. I've been over the scene a million times in my mind. It's the only way they could've gotten her out there without leaving tracks."

The same as I've suspected at other scenes though I can't tell him that. "We're in a city full of winged children of the gods."

"We are."

"From what I've heard, everyone here can fly except the Huntresses and the Styx."

"I wouldn't be too sure about the Styx," he says. "Never underestimate women who can navigate the waters of the dead."

"Which means literally anyone in Syn City except the Huntresses could be a suspect."

"Unless your office has been behind the killings all along." He makes the accusation sound so matter-of-fact. "The murders have taken out targets that weaken every alpha. I don't trust the marshals. No one species should be in charge of all the packs."

"We're not looking to take over or lead."

"Uh huh." He stares at me as if he's waiting for my nose to grow Pinocchio-style. Or he's picking a body part of mine to punch. "None of us are safe until the killers are caught. Come on. I'll get your evidence for you."

I follow him and glance at the rows of blades lining his walls, wondering who I can trust in this town except my wolf already knows even if my human half doesn't want to hear it.

Sadie.

12

SADIE

THE RINK'S AN OPEN PLAYGROUND TODAY FOR ALL THE HOUSES. Muses fly from spotlight to spotlight, Nymphs zip in the air above the stands, and the Mad Maes dance drunkenly above the skating track. Which leaves me and my sisters skating for fun with the Gorgons—wings out.

Tisia skates next to me, wearing a different Hack and Ale shirt today. Her split lip has scabbed, and a dark bruise covers part of her face. "Hate I missed makeovers and manicures last night. I hear you put on quite the show."

I shake my head. "They came for free samples of product my brand releases next spring, not for me."

"Still, it probably helped argue the case this morning to the Syndicate that you had zero connection to any supposed jailbreak by the marshal and me."

"Freaking Huntresses. They didn't have the right to lock either of you up." I dodge a basketball game with the net forty feet in the air and no penalties for wings or fouls.

"They wouldn't show their faces at the open rink after that judgment. Not when they'd be the only wingless ones here." She snickers. "Except the Styx and those dead bitches wouldn't know how to cut loose and have a good time. Why isn't your marshal here?"

"He's not my marshal."

"*Suuure*. Except Bunny mentioned she scented you on him."

"What? When?" That rabbit.

"When she was helping Stone bust me out last night."

"No." I flare my wings. "I mean when did she sniff him?"

"Jealous?" Leave it to Tisia to make me ask such ridiculous questions.

"No. What he does is none of my business." Except if I'm still imagining freaking colors the next time I see him, I'll wring his wolf neck. "Kiva said he was supposed to head out this morning on a seaplane."

"The Syndicate allowed that?" Her shock mirrors my own from earlier. "Aircraft haven't been authorized to fly near Syn City in years."

"They let a marshal come to town. What the hell difference will a plane make?"

"True. But he's your marshal." Tisia makes kissing noises.

"Don't make me gag."

"Your sisters seem happy with their mates." She lifts her chin toward where Kiva battles Stone with foam swords they obviously swiped from the merch booths while Dottie plays flirty tag with Chase in his mountain lion form bounding over the rows of chairs. Both my sisters use their wings to their advantage.

"They are. But I'm not meant to be a marshal's mate." I try not to think of his off-handed comment about going back to Nashville with him. As if I could.

"He could get a new job."

"The marshal's office is his life, has been since before I turned Fury. It's his purpose, the same as seeking revenge for my family is mine. If we're lucky we can help each other out before we go our separate ways."

"That sucks." Bumping into me, she says, "Hey, maybe you

two can scratch a wolfy itch before he goes." She waggles her brows.

"You're bad."

"I'm the worst." She grins and hardly flinches when the movement pulls at her wounds. The woman's derby tough. Her smile falls, and she jerks her head toward the mid-level deck where the main entries open to outside. Devlyn and the Huntresses walk in. "Looks like I jinxed sexy times for everybody. What are the prude police doing here?"

I manage not to blush. While I don't go around judging people's sex lives like the Huntresses do, I'm no more experienced than they are. That's what I get for crushing on a wolf who's married to the marshal service and more interested in what good I might be in solving a big case that'll land him a promotion than seeing me for *me*. "No idea. I thought they'd be pouting over the Syndicate's decision."

"I still don't know what happened at the bar yesterday, but they've shut the Hack and Ale down indefinitely."

"Sorry, Tisia."

"Not your fault. The whole damn city has gone crazy." She seems to be counting the green uniforms with her pointer finger and not on the sly. "The two who were practicing their archery at the bar when all hell broke loose? They're not here."

"You think the Huntresses put their own teammates on time out?" I ask.

"Wouldn't surprise me after the stupidity they pulled yesterday. Locking me in the arcade and then telling me they'd give me time to cool off before they questioned me. Cool off from what? And why'd they take off for hours? I'm just glad Bunny keeps master keys to open any door in the city."

Devlyn and the Huntresses head our way, changing into skates and circling the lap like it's no big deal they're here after yesterday's stunt. Or that it's normal they're the only women on the track without wings.

I glance their way, then back to the Gorgon they wronged.

Tisia shakes her head. "It's not worth starting something over. Not yet anyway."

I don't get a chance to ask her *then when* because an eerie silence descends over The Rink. The clack of skates and flap of wings go quiet.

A line of white-robed Styx circle the mid-level, their matching blank masks a scary reminder that they know exactly what happens when we Furies reach the end of our second shots at life. The sight gives me shivers. Whispers swirl around us, and even the Mad Maes stop their twirling and drunken giggles.

"There's been a death," Tisia says softly. "Had to have been to get them to come above ground for something other than an official Syndicate-mandated gig."

"Or there's about to be," I agree. The last time the Styx gathered there'd been the imminent threat of death involving several children victims who'd almost drowned. My stomach sinks. *Please don't let them be here about a kid.*

Dread spirals through me, spinning as much as the other House members on skates circling to score a better look at the Styx or find out what's going on.

Maizie and the other coaches move to the infield. I know by the curious expressions around me that I'm not the only one who's shamelessly eavesdropping. Seconds crawl by with agonizing slowness while we wait.

In the stands, Bunny rushes toward Stone and Chase. After I get over the oddness of watching prey run *toward* predators instead of away from them, the truth hits me. Stone puts one big hand on Bunny's shoulder and Chase rubs his lion shifter self against her as if offering comfort.

"Whoever died? They were a shifter," I whisper to Tisia.

"You sure your marshal left on a plane this morning?"

My head pounds, and my stomach threatens to revolt. "I was until you asked that." I don't even question her calling Nolan *mine*. Right now, I want more than anything for him to cowboy swagger into The Rink and appear between Styx robes.

Maizie takes to the air. "Everyone back to your Houses. That is your coaches' decision. Furies, do not leave your triads."

I stall, waiting for my sisters to tell their shifter mates goodbye since their men insist on walking a heartbroken Bunny back to the staff quarters.

Hours later, Nolan still hasn't shown. My sisters and I check on my garden as best we can with the Huntresses watching our every move. I won't tip them off to the garden's location.

"Come on," Dottie says. "We'll go wait near the swamp's edge and see if we can spy the plane coming back."

I appreciate her not making a big deal out of me missing Nolan. "Won't matter much with the Huntresses itching to haul him in for questioning again." But we go anyway because my restlessness worries my sisters.

Our swamp doesn't hold the same brimstone sulfur and decaying rot stench of most marshes. It's more citrus, cypress, and sweetness thanks to the immortal magic. The moon shines on the water yet the inky blackness swallows it instead of shimmering silver. The low hum of frogs and crickets comes from the woods. None would risk getting too close to the gators, harpies, and sea hags that populate our swamp.

When Stone and Chase come to check on their mates, I give them privacy by waiting at the water's edge.

The roar of a seaplane has me glancing skyward. I haven't seen an airplane in years. Sure, I've heard about how big commercial jets flew everywhere before the Witching Wars, before spotty electricity and tech had so many dropping out of the skies. Small planes and helicopters fared better in rural areas where the threat of collision was less. We even had a few fly over Nashville for military purposes or for the rare person who could afford the sky-high fuel prices without a care for their safety. But a barely-lit little plane that drops out of the sky and into the water? If he's riding in that, Nolan has either no fear or no sense. *Gods, I hope he's in there.*

"Marshal's back," Stone says. With the noise of the plane, I didn't hear the grizzly shifter sneak up on me.

"Looks like." So much for a smart comeback. "Any word on who we lost?" I use the term *we* when a week ago, I wouldn't have considered a shifter other than my sisters' mates to be much of a loss. How fast some things change.

"A wild boar sow visiting on a student-work visa from England. She was a pack chieftain's youngest daughter. I didn't know her, but she and Bunny had become friends."

When I'd offered my condolences to Bunny, she stared at me as if I had spoken a dead language. Of course, I spent the last three years pushing anger onto any shifter who crossed my path, and now I learn that I blamed Lowell for something he didn't do.

"Same as the other shifters?" I don't want details. I know them all too well from my own murder scene.

"Exact same except no arrowhead. Or at least none that they found."

"The killer's here in Syn City." I hate knowing whoever killed me and my family is out there free and still causing pain to other people's loved ones.

"Or they were." Stone doesn't elaborate. "If Nolan got out today, the killer could have too, and we don't know how long the sow's been dead. Could be minutes. Could be hours. Only an autopsy by someone used to dealing with shifter healing will tell us. Do me a favor. My woman thinks the world of you, and she has lost all the family she ever had except you, Dottie, and me. Stay safe. Don't let her lose you too."

"I can do that," I promise.

"You good this close to the swamp and the sea hags?" He stares over the water and its stillness that hides so much.

"The sea hags don't scare me. We're kin of sorts." The spirits of women suspected of witchcraft, the sea hags were killed by humans—whether they'd practiced any spellcraft or not. "Another time or place, and I could've been one of them."

"But you have your kin right here in your sisters. Chase and me too if you'll have us. More importantly, you're a Fury needing revenge. If Nolan's right, you'll get it."

"If he solves the case before we're all kicked out of Syn City for the Huntresses to turn it into their own private shooting preserve."

"We have days yet to fight that battle. Let's just get through tonight." He turns to head back toward Kiva, stops, and looks at me. "The marshal asked for your help. You willing to give it to him?"

Do I want to remember whatever it is that my mind might have blocked to protect me? No. But will I try? "Yeah. I'll do whatever it takes to stop this insanity."

Stone walks away, and I stay alone where the ground meets the water among the cattails and lilies that shouldn't have the fluorescent glow that they do when the moon hits them just right. A sea hag glides through the water toward the shore. I don't move. As I told Stone, the hags invoke a lot of feelings for me but not fear.

According to the legends, she can't see, but she can hear. Perhaps she can sense me the same way I do her. With long, stringy, dark hair and a greyish face, I wonder how she looked in *her* first life. Had she been tan-skinned like my sister Hazel or as fair as my mother? Did she enjoy working with plants the way I do? Or cooking love into her spells the same as she did her suppers? I sit and stare at her, searching for answers that I don't really want. Because if my family's here, if my mother or sisters are here, no amount of revenge will be enough to give them justice.

A shimmering blue orb floats over the water, and I glance behind me. Nolan holds another magical light in his hand, the swirling green resting above his palm. "Neat trick the Nymphs have with their glow balls. They offered me a shiny stick to go with them." He snickers. Men.

"Of course the Nymphs turn sacred powers into dick jokes."

"They seem sweet enough but like I said, not my type." He stares at the water. "Is that a sea hag?" His hand goes to his weapon. Stupid wolf. Still carrying a firearm in a deity daughter town.

"Don't bother her, and she won't bother you. At least not while I'm here."

"I heard they drag their victims to the bottom of the swamp and drown them so they'll have company."

"They used to be humans. Or witches. Maybe a bit of both."

He steps next to me, his boots almost touching the water. "Like you?"

"Exactly like me." I don't give him time to ask more questions about that. "Besides, we both know you're more scared of itty bitty snakes than real monsters."

"Woman, you're mean enough that a snake wouldn't dare slither this way just to bite me."

His low chuckle works a kind of magic on me that has nothing to do with spells or witches. I glance up at him, the way his strong jaw and whiskey eyes reflect in the light, and I'm so glad he's here and safe. That he wasn't the one the killer went after. No matter how selfish or insensitive that makes me. I can't lose anyone else. "Don't you dare die on me," I whisper.

"Same." There's a brokenness to his voice, a vulnerability I haven't heard before. "You've already done it once. I can't live through it again."

It's time to let go of old resentments, fears, and the crap ton of emotional baggage that comes with it. "Let's see if we can knock some memories loose and find my killer."

13

NOLAN

Sadie by the water shouldn't stir *everything* in me, but it does. Finding her here soothed the fear I've had in the hours since I heard about the latest murder. My wolf has paced with the need to see her, and my fox wanted to say screw the investigation and get back to our mate. This many personalities fighting for space within me is exhausting, and I'll be wiped before I can sleep again with knowing I let another shifter down.

"What do you mean knock your memories loose?" I ask. "You don't remember the murder." Or at least that's what she told me. Had she lied?

"The therapist who treats the Furies." She stops and gives me a *don't judge* look. "I mean the Syndicate pays her to consult with all seven Houses, but she says we need her most."

I'm not judging in the least. Hell, I'm glad they have someone on staff who's trained to deal with trauma. "Makes sense given that every one of you was a murder victim."

"She says I might be repressing some of my memories about that day." Again, she stares at the water instead of going on with the explanation, and the worry coming off her in waves through the mating bond doesn't surprise me.

"I would block every memory of that day if I could, and I was only there for the aftermath."

"Dr. Bomani thinks she can test the theory through memory regression. I might not get everything back, but we could attempt it."

"You haven't before?"

She shakes her head.

"That means you had a good reason not to," I say before she thinks I'm questioning her decision. "Is it dangerous?"

"Shouldn't be."

If I hadn't known her for years, I might've missed the tells in her expression that scream she just lied to me—the tightening around her eyes, the tiny tug downward of her lips, the fact she's staring at the sea hag as if that ugly monster holds the secrets to life. "Yeah, that's not reassuring. Try telling me the truth this time."

"It could take a few sessions, or it might not work at all. Dr. Bomani would attempt it at her office. So physically, I'd be safe."

But mentally she'd be a wreck. I don't like thinking of her going through that even though it's literally the reason I met with her as soon as I arrived in Syn City, to force her to cooperate with the investigation. Now the thought makes my stomach twist in a sick feeling that I don't want to examine too much. "Does this doctor use magic or something?"

"No, we learned the hard way that magic twists things. Kiva had a witch plant false memories that nearly convinced her that her mate had killed her. Dr. Bomani wouldn't let that happen."

"You trust this doctor?"

"Kiva does, and she tends to be a harsh judge of people. All of us Furies are...except Dottie."

The woman would have to be laid back to mate with a freakin' cat. "Butterfly Wings loves everyone, huh?"

"Pretty much." She glances at me, and I swear her green eyes take on a shine in this light. "Come with me?"

It takes a full second for the weight of what she's asking to sink in. "You want me to stay with you in the doctor's office?"

"Yeah." Her voice goes rough, and the fact that my strong mate is reduced to near tears—it guts me. She goes back to staring at the water. "If it helps with the investigation, great. If not, then we'll both know. Either way, you should be there. We both could use the closure as Dr. Bomani would say."

Which is how I find myself in a shrink's office the next day for the first time outside of visits required by the marshal's office. Those happened in a beige-walled office with no windows, a cheap aluminum table, and two chairs that wouldn't be missed if a shifter went ballistic and destroyed everything in the room. A consultant would ask questions from a form, follow up with the standard *do you want to talk about that*, and either sign off on our fitness for duty or commit us to a lockdown facility. We marshals don't work with partners so I didn't care about the low standards, especially when it allowed me to avoid topics like my family.

But now, in a welcoming room with wide windows that have sunlight streaming through, couches and chairs that might be someone's living room, and a cozy setup for tea and coffee that could be grandma's house—if grandma wasn't a big, bad wolf—I'm glad Sadie has a professional to talk with who seems to have a genuine interest in her wellbeing.

The doc gives me a pointed look and says, "You can stay as long as she's comfortable with that arrangement. The moment Sadie changes her mind, you're out, marshal or not. Don't speak unless asked. This isn't your session."

I sink into a chair so plush that I would fall asleep if my every nerve wasn't pinging from an adrenaline rush. The doctor looks human. Yet she doesn't smell like it. Below the scents of lemons and fabric softener, I get an overwhelming hit of feline.

At first, I wonder if the subtle artwork featuring lions on the throw pillows, the rug, and an abstract painting has tricked my senses. But no...the cat scent's coming from the brown-skinned woman with black hair shot through with enough grey to make me think she's in her fifties. Or she would be if she was human. Staring at her doesn't go over well. No matter that her gaze has been pinned on Sadie, she gives me a look that says to stop studying her and pay attention to her patient.

"Nolan's fairly harmless," Sadie tells her. "Except when he picked on me mercilessly after my fifteenth birthday."

"Fifteen, hmm?" The next glance the doctor shoots my way says she knows exactly why my attitude toward Sadie changed. "He's a wolf marshal so while he's not as dangerous as you, I'm sure he knows how to do more than shoot that gun he shouldn't be wearing in Syn City."

"I've told him that," Sadie says on a sigh, but at least she's not poking at the fifteenth birthday thing.

I replay the doc's words in my mind. She acknowledges the threat I present with my training and my shifter strength and speed yet she believes Sadie's the bigger badass. While I haven't seen her fight, she has always been tough, and I like knowing she can defend herself. The vigilante side of her wanting to take on her killer? I'm less thrilled about that.

"I'm sure you have." Dr. Bomani has a soothing voice, one that could coax an injured pup out of hiding. But she doesn't patronize. "What changed your mind about looking into your past?"

"Talking to Nolan. He says I fought whoever killed me. I don't remember that."

"And you believe him?" The doc tosses out the accusation that I could've lied so casually that it's hard to get mad about it. Worse, I need to hear Sadie's answer.

"Yes." She glances at me. "He might not have spared my feelings in the past, and he doesn't always tell the whole truth, but he hasn't lied to me." Crossing one black-clad leg over the other in a *swish* of fabric and slide of leather as those *fuck me* stiletto boots slip one against the other, she focuses on the doctor again. "How do we do this? Can I stay sitting up or do I have to lie on the couch? Are you going to hypnotize me?"

"Stay as you are if you like. Or move around if you need to." The doctor waves her hand toward the open space behind the couch. "I don't practice the Freudian techniques so there will be no hypnosis. First, you tell me the facts as you remember them now in as much detail as you can provide."

"And then?" Sadie asks.

"Then, I'll ask the marshal to wait in the hall a few moments while I ease you into a relaxed state—for his safety in case your Fury side rebels. When you're secure in the knowledge that this is a safe place to explore those memories, I'll invite him to return, and we will see if you remember anything more. There is no guarantee of unlocking memories that your mind may have repressed to protect you."

Sadie bites at her bottom lip, the red lipstick stark against her white teeth. I want to kiss those lips, hold her against me and tell her she's safe, take her out of here and away from her past, but I can't. Not if we want to catch the killer before they figure out she's my best way to find them. Before they come after her. So I stay put and force my wolf to watch her push past fear that only she can face.

"One more question," she says.

"Ask as many as you need." The doctor's calm voice suggests she'll take as long as necessary to answer.

"What if I'm stuck with not remembering?" Sadie asks. "Like Kiva?"

"Not that I'm discussing my other patients, but your Fury sister had amnesia caused by a curse. As far as we know, that's not the case with you."

"All right." Sadie rubs her hands against her thighs. "Let's get started."

Listening to the details of the screams Sadie heard, the terror she felt, the panic she overcame to push herself up those stairs to find a protective spell to save her family? It makes my chest squeeze tight, my mouth go dry, and my stomach knot as if I've swallowed rocks.

Worse—hearing how she blames herself for murders that she couldn't have stopped? It fucking tears me up inside. I should've listened to Lowell's concerns that someone had followed him to her family home. I should've done more to protect him...and her. I should be the one carrying whatever guilt she feels, heaped atop my own.

When Dr. Bomani asks me to step into the hall, I jump at the chance to take a moment and a deep breath, to get my shit together. Separating my emotions from this case has never been possible, but now, I'm so tied up with worry and regret about my mate that logic takes a backseat to our incomplete bond.

"You can come in now," Dr. Bomani says. "I don't care what information we do or don't obtain for your investigation. Sadie's wellbeing is my concern. She's under a mild tranquility spell but remains in full control. If she pushes anywhere near her limits, I'm stopping. We clear?"

I've done this to my mate. "I understand."

She studies me as if she can peer inside my head. "I think maybe you do." Taking her seat, she curls like a freakin' cat in the rocking chair near my woman, and what the hell is wrong with Sadie? She's staring as if she's...happy. Like she's blissed out on her mom's calming cookies. I can't see the colors coming off our mating bond.

"What'd you do to her?" I bark. "I thought you said no hypnosis."

"Sit," Dr. Bomani snaps at me as though I'm a dog. She gives me a mischievous grin with no malice. I do what she says without thinking. Maybe she slipped me some of her magical calming mojo too because I'm suddenly not as worried anymore. "Now Sadie, you said you wanted to start at the staircase to the attic when you went to get the grimoire. Do you still wish to use that focal point?"

Sadie nods. "That's right."

"This is a safe place," the doctor tells her. "Whatever you saw or heard on the staircase, it's in the past, and it will remain in the past. Nothing can harm you here. You'll feel no actual pain, and you will stop before your first life ended. If you decide at any time to return to the present, you'll do so immediately. Do you understand?"

"Yes." Sadie stares into the distance. "I'm on the stairs, and I keep sliding. Mud and blood make my feet slippery. My fingers can't twist the door knob. Something sharp stuck me in the back, and my hand doesn't work anymore."

I curl my hands into fists, wanting to beat whoever hurt her and wishing like hell that I hadn't brought this fight back to her doorstep.

"You're safe," the doctor reminds her. "No pain can reach you here."

Sadie shakes her head. "I must reach the grimoire. A protective spell's my family's last chance. They've already broken through our wards."

"Who?" I blurt out before I can stop myself.

The doctor blasts me with a pulse of power that has me squirming in my seat. *What* is she?

"They have wings." Sadie's voice pitches high, and her whole body lights with ribbons of grey, red, and black spooling from her. "I can't, I won't—I'm failing them. I fall and the shadows chase me."

"That's enough." The doctor waves her hand, and Sadie slumps back against the couch cushions. "You'll remember only the visions. Not the pain, not the fear, not the ugliness beyond that of the past which already plagues you. This I promise."

Rubbing at her forehead, my mate sits up, the colors around

her fading as if she wrapped a shielding blanket around herself. "I'm all right," she says.

"Do you want to talk about what you've remembered?" the doctor asks.

"I can keep going." Sadie's words slow with exhaustion, her shoulders slumping no matter how stiffly she holds her spine.

I don't care if the doctor blasts me again. "No, you're done."

"For once I have to agree with him," Dr. Bomani says. "We can discuss what you remembered and the emotions it stirred up, and you can hold anything else for later."

"If I want to wait, we can?" Sadie asks.

"That's your choice. Not mine. You don't need my permission." She follows Sadie's gaze to me. "Nor his."

"Please say we're done for today," I say. I can't watch her suffer anymore.

Sadie cracks a smile, and I swear it takes a sledgehammer to my heart. My mate's suffering yet she would put the investigation above herself if I asked. "Wuss," she calls me.

"Stubborn."

She doesn't miss a beat. "Meanie."

"Smarty pants."

"Hard-headed."

"Fair enough," I concede.

Dr. Bomani stands and heads for the door. "Let's save couples' therapy for another time, shall we?"

I don't tell her she's wrong. Hell, maybe *I* have been wrong about this whole mating connection. If the marshals could move me closer, I could spend the rest of my life trying to be the man that my mate deserves. She might not have to know that I'm a fox's bastard. Or knowing Sadie, she'd say being one kind of shifter's no better than another. The woman can keep secrets, that's for sure. And what a woman.

She stands and wobbles on those heels that could double as

ice picks. I offer her my arm, expecting her to scowl or slap at me. To my surprise, she takes it.

"Come on," she says, "I know a place we can go to work out our differences."

Dear gods, I don't care if she's talking about a bed, a wall, a freakin' rock in the middle of her poison garden, so long as she lets me kiss her again.

14

SADIE

"Nymphs shouting at each other and jabbing their spears in the air," Nolan says. "This was your idea of working out differences?"

He sits next to me by the flames. His auburn hair catches glints of the firelight, shining copper and gold, and I want to trace the freckles on his cheek. Instead, I'm bandaging the cut on his forehead. "Fight training works out a lot of issues. It's not the Hack and Ale, but it's still a party."

"As long as it gets your mind off the memories, we'll call the evening a win." He presses his back against the outside wall of Stone's forge like he's the iron holding the damn place up. "Hell, you didn't even make any of the pigtails cry when you beat them all at stick fighting."

"But they made you cry," I tease although I'm not sure how he managed not to tear up when a Nymph missed the mark he was holding for her by a good three feet and smacked him square in the nuts. Not to mention the prior jabs to his chest and gut. When he ducked to grab his balls, she clobbered him in the head. Thus, the cut I'm patching.

He grunts, and I swear he packs a wallop of feeling in the sound. Hell, he'll probably be black and blue tomorrow, and the Fates shame me, but I sort of want to take a peek. Before I can let my brain go too far on that thought, he says, "Let's hope the world never needs the pigtails to save it because we'll all be doomed."

"I don't know. She took you out pretty easily." I dab on more antiseptic. Is the wound clean? Yeah, but I like watching him squirm.

He hisses. "Ow, what are you using to clean that scratch? Battery acid?"

"You never know what STD might jump off a Nymph onto you." I switch to a soothing salve that I keep stocked at Stone's school because no regular first aid kit will suffice when Gorgons and Furies decide to beat the crap out of each other with training weapons. "Any known allergies other than wolf's bane?"

He eyes me suspiciously. "Why do you ask?"

"Relax, if I'd wanted to poison you, you'd be dead already. The salves stocked here are shifter safe."

"For all shifters?"

Weird that he wants to know since he's a boring old wolf, but... "Yeah. Not that it matters. Every shifter species is the same in the end—part human, part beast, all a pain in my ass."

"You really feel that way?"

"I don't rank shifter species like you wolves do although I don't see you treating me different now that I'm not human with witch tendencies."

"You're the same *you* as a Fury with the same witchy ways except faster, stronger, and more deadly which makes you—"

"A bloodthirsty psychopath?" I wondered when we would get to this conversation.

"Harder to kill." He meets my gaze, and there's respect shining there. "Which I appreciate."

I did *not* expect that. Worse, I'm momentarily speechless.

Taking my time putting a sparkly purple Muse bandage on his forehead, I do my best to hide any emotions because nothing has come off of him when he looks at me since my session with Dr. Bomani except beautiful threads of gold. I clear my throat. "Why be nice to me now? You gave back the grimoire. I agreed to help you. You have nothing to gain from pretending we're friends."

"Oh, we're not friends."

Now he tells me. I should've left the cut on his head to fester and swell. I shut the salve with a snap.

"Wait." He touches my hand, trailing his fingers along mine. "I didn't mean it like that."

"Then how did you mean it? You're amazing for four years and the best influence a kid could have. I turn fifteen and *poof!* You criticize everything on the rare occasions you bother to notice me. You take things from my family home without bothering to contact me for three years, and now—"

"I'm sorry."

His apology catches me off guard, and I sit with a hard *thunk*. "About?" My throat goes dry. Nolan doesn't do regrets or remorse.

He strokes a thumb over my knuckles. "For being a dick to you. For not reaching out sooner. For not protecting you and your family."

Shit got heavy real quick. My stomach twists in a boulder-sized knot. "You couldn't have protected us. They got past security wards and Lowell." They would've come through Nolan too. I leave the last unsaid because I *can't* say it. I can barely think it.

"Yet you think you should've stopped them."

My brain flashes to the instinctive *well, yeah* that I've dwelled on for years, but something in his tone stops me from saying it out loud. "You couldn't have saved them either. Their deaths weren't your fault."

"But I—"

"You *died*, Sadie. Those fuckers killed you, and you fought until the end." He squeezes my hand as if he needs to hold onto me. "Lowell said he'd been followed. He didn't want me to say anything because his position as the alpha's son—"

"The same as you." I can't understand why Nolan and his dad didn't get along.

"Not the same," he says. "Not at all. Lowell didn't want me looking into it. Thought it'd make him seem weak or paranoid. But better if people had thought that than him winding up..."

"Dead. He fought back too. And what could you have done? Trailed your younger brother everywhere?"

"I could've requested a protective detail to be assigned to Lowell. Asked the marshals to find out who followed him."

"The wolf marshals aren't known for being kind or helpful. They probably would've said no, you and Lowell would've been branded cowards, and wolves couldn't have taken on *flying* killers anyway."

"Could've shot the fuckers out of the sky."

"And if they'd been deity daughters—more exist in the world than just the seven Houses of Syn City—you'd have brought curses down on every marshal who opened fire."

"But the threat's been in *this* town. It might still be here now," he says. "Murdering a poor shifter who came here to work and learn. If I had solved the case sooner, she'd still be alive. So would the deer alpha's daughters and the bobcat grandma."

"The victims from nearby towns?"

"Yeah. I've questioned everyone close to them, analyzed the crime scenes, and know that the same killer or killers have committed each. But who?" He shakes his head as if trying to clear it, and I wonder how hard the Nymph smacked him in the skull. "The wings..." He stops himself. "I know you don't want to talk about what you remembered in Dr. Bomani's office, and I'm not asking. I just keep thinking the witness statements I got from prior investigations are missing critical information."

"Like?"

"Like Stone saying that whoever dumped the cub's body on the ice had to have flown her in. No one from the marshal's interviewed the bears, and they sure as hell didn't talk to Stone. I don't even have a record of Kiva's death. I wouldn't have known except she's your Fury sister, and her mate was willing to talk to me. Likely because of my connection to you. He has no love for the marshals."

Stone's patiently teaching a Nymph how *not* to hold her spear like a little leaguer getting ready to take a swing at her first tee ball game. Releasing her chokehold on the weapon, the woman's blue and silver wings shimmer like ocean waves in motion. They're so peaceful and lovely. So unlike the wings in my memories. "If those memories I had in Dr. Bomani's office were true"—since she warned us both of the possibility that false memories could surface—"I haven't seen wings like those of my killer's in this second life as a Fury."

"Did you see any faces?"

"No, just the one set of wings. I knew there were multiple attackers in the house, that I needed to get to the attic, but I didn't remember more detail. Not yet anyway."

"Tell me about the wings you've seen here in Syn City." He glances at the Nymph, takes a draw off the bottle of honey beer that he swiped from Stone's fridge, and looks at me. "Yours are stunning."

Not the descriptor I would've expected. Scary? Witchy? Freaky? Sure. But stunning? "Wings match the colors of their Houses. Ours are black." I nod toward the Nymph. "Theirs come in all shades of blue. The Muses' wings range from deep purple to almost magenta. The ones I saw before I died? They could've been tree branches stretched out and stripped of their leaves."

"Creepy."

"Yeah." A chill runs through me, spreading goosebumps across my skin. "Or bones." The thought has my chest going tight.

"Wings made of bone. My baby sister drew something like that in her book of shadows."

"I saw it, but didn't know what to make of it," he admits. "Your mom said Mabel had promise of becoming a great Seer."

"Mabel had visions of the future. Sometimes she saw happy ones, but most gave her nightmares. What if she saw our deaths?"

He doesn't answer, just stares at the Nymphs as though he's processing the awful possibility.

Kiva lands with a thump in the middle of the sparring Nymphs, sending them scattering. She glances my way with simmering rage in her eyes. I hurry her direction.

"The Syndicate passed a ruling on the riot," she says. "They decided the madness at the Hack and Ale was induced by drugs slipped in the bar snacks and triggered by the scream of a wild boar."

I can't believe it. "They're blaming the murdered shifter?"

She nods. "The sow. Who didn't have any history of violence."

"It makes no sense. No shifter scream can do that." With Nashville considered a city where humans and supernaturals lived together, my junior high science class covered shifter basics from animal coexistence to enhanced speed, strength, and healing. "That's the stuff of gods or real magic slingers."

Kiva gives a derisive snort. "We know the magic wielders aren't leaving their sanctuaries. So unless the poor woman had a war-invoking squeal or hid a monstrous other side—"

"Like the Calydonian boar," the Nymph who strangled her spear the same as a baseball bat says.

"The what now?" Kiva asks and looks at me.

"I have no idea." I glance at the Nymph whose wings practically vibrate as if she's excited she can add to the conversation.

"From Greek mythology." She hands her spear to Stone when he reaches for it, saying it was better than chancing she might stick herself with it. "You know, the legend of the Calydonian boar hunt."

"Can't say that I know that bedtime story," Kiva says.

Me neither. While we're deity daughters, Syn City doesn't give a basic *learn the ancient bullshit of your immortal parents* course. We sort of wing it—no pun intended—with the mission handed to us by our creators.

The Nymph grins. "Once upon a time—"

"I don't think that's how myths start," Kiva says.

"Shush," I tell her. "Let her spin the wild pig legend however she wants as long as she covers the key points. Go ahead."

"Once upon a time," the Nymph starts again, "a dreadful boar rampaged across the countryside, terrifying the people and devastating the land. The monster roared thunder and belched lightning that scorched the earth."

"Okay," Kiva says, "I call bullshit."

Glaring at her, I point out the obvious. "We died and came back to life able to fly and call magical weapons into our hand with a simple thought. Myths are grounded in magic so suspend reality for a minute...or an hour if you don't quit interrupting her." I gesture for the Nymph to continue.

"It's true," she insists. "The boar's mother was a murderous sow, the sister of monsters such as the hydra and chimera."

I wave a hand. "I believe you. Skip the *who begat whom* part and get to the action."

"Okay." She nods, her blue pigtails bouncing. "A bunch of heroes got together and slew the beast."

"This story blows," Kiva mutters.

"Did the legend say why the monster pig attacked everyone?" I ask. "Who sent it or doomed it or whatever?"

"Oh, that's easy," she says brightly. "A human king only honored eleven of the twelve big gods when he presented his rites and offerings. Pissed because he forgot her, Artemis sent the boar."

"Who?" Nolan asks, coming up behind me.

"Artemis." The Nymph sounds out the word as if he's stupid.

"Goddess of chastity, wild animals, and the hunt." She pauses like she's waiting for any of us to say *oh yeah, that Artemis.* When we don't, she adds, "Mother of the Huntresses. You know, the green-wearing snobs who run around thinking *our mother's better than yours since she's an Olympian goddess and not some lesser god or demigod like a nymph or muse or fury?*"

"Oh." I feel like she has just served us on our ignorance. Who knew the Nymphs were scholars on top of being flirts? "Have the Huntresses ever said outright that their mom is this Artemis?"

"Well, no but duh. Look at their actual House."

"No one has seen inside," Kiva says.

"No, but the outside could be a replica of an ancient temple with its marble columns. Plus, they use bow and arrows like Artemis. And they're big on using stag antlers, goat horns, and forest patterns in their décor."

"Where'd you learn all this?" I ask. "Furies are more about training to skate and kill than library learning."

The Nymph shrugs. "I watch history holograms to help me sleep. Some of it sticks."

"Anything in the myths have wings that look like bones?" I ask her, glancing at Nolan.

"No, not that I recall."

That's good enough for me. It's definitely time to look outside Syn City for the killer. Maybe other deities have sent their sons and daughters to stir up trouble. Magic didn't just bring back the Greek gods and goddesses. Several ancient cultures have resurrected their deities. "Thanks for the help," I tell her.

Nolan's phone lights up. "It's my boss," he whispers before answering. "Captain Zaleski—" His brow furrows. "Yes, ma'am. I'll see you soon." He hangs up, and the damn dark colors that come off him make me want to slug whoever made him this upset.

"What's wrong?"

He shoves the phone in his pocket and curls his hand into a

fist. "My captain's coming to town. They've moved up my deadline. I only have a week to solve the case."

"We need more than luck, visions, and a few days to catch a killer." I swipe his bottle of beer and take a long swig. "We're going to need a gods damned miracle."

15

NOLAN

ANOTHER DAY WASTED, AND I'M NO CLOSER TO FIGURING OUT WHO keeps killing shifters or why. So I do the only thing that makes sense and follow the mating connection to Sadie's garden.

She presses a utility knife against my throat before I can say hello.

"Holy Hades! Nolan, I could've killed you." Her surprise at least means she didn't intend to attack *me* specifically, just whoever wandered this way.

"Nah, I figured it was only foreplay to get us back to the kissing."

"Foreplay?" She has her hair pulled up in a bun on top of her head like a ballerina with a few blonde strands falling around her face. The sinking sun casts a halo of gold and rose around her. Her mouth is painted with bright pink lipstick that looks as out of place in the garden as the skirt she's wearing and the big ass sword propped against a stone. "You're awfully ambitious."

"A man needs hope."

She sheaths the knife. "I'm guessing you didn't get anywhere on the investigation today. I sure as hell didn't. I visited Dr. Bomani again, but we didn't find anything new. The Syndicate has put all blame on the murdered shifter. Poppy was her name, and other than her parents naming her Poppy the pig, I found nothing criminal in her past or her family's. Nice girl. Lovely manners. Very neat and tidy. Not anyone I suspect of inciting panic. You?"

"Captain Zaleski arrives tomorrow, and I've nothing to show her but another dead shifter." Which means I'll lose my badge in a week, but I'm not telling Sadie that. She has enough to worry over.

"What's the Syndicate trying to cover up?" she asks.

"I don't know. I appreciate them letting me out of further questioning and cooperating with the investigation but blaming a shifter doesn't solve anything."

"The fighting in the streets the other night left a couple of broken bones and a few stitches. A mean derby bout could cause the same level of injuries. But if *all* the Houses broke into a panic like that? We'd be carting off bodies."

Not a mental image either of us needs. "Because I don't want that to happen, I called my archives expert. Figured I could get info on Artemis as well as this feral pig panic thing."

"Your expert tell you anything useful?"

I rub at the stress ache that has kept my head pounding all day. "Only that the Nymph was mostly right about what she remembered from the history holograms. Other deities used bows and arrows. Some from Greek mythology, others from different parts of the word. A few in Africa, a Norse god, one in China, another warrior goddess in India. Plus, all the Amazons."

"Our silver arrowhead doesn't narrow it as much as we'd like?"

"Not at all. Those are just the deities or mythological legends that practice archery. Who knows how many followers of other religions or just crazy weapons enthusiasts have carved weird shit into silver arrows and called them sacred?"

"She tell you anything else? About the chaos not being caused by Poppy the peaceful pig."

I don't comment on the fact that she's defending a shifter in her own snarky way. "Maenads can start orgies and ecstasy-driven insanity, but not panic. That comes from the Greek god Pan, a satyr half-man, half-goat who screwed everything he could catch."

"Past tense?" she asks. "Since when does someone talk about an immortal that way?"

"He's the only god on record to have been reported as dead."

"So we have a copycat of a dead god on top of serial killers? How could those be connected?"

"No idea," I admit, not adding the other gods of fear and panic that all ran together in my head. "But if we figure out the link, maybe we solve the case." Which would get my captain and the upper brass to stop threatening my badge long enough that I could try to work through things with Sadie.

"Still think this is linked to my murder and my family's? To whoever had those weird wings made of bone?"

"Yeah, I do. I've hunted every witness I could find that the marshals hadn't interviewed yet. Every crime scene has no sign of tracks, no footprints, no way in or out. Each had a dumped body that someone had to fly in—except for your family's home which came first in time."

"You think the killers started with us?"

I nod because I can't stand to say another word that puts such a haunted look in her gaze.

She walks away, wiping the dirt from her hands.

As a kid, I once brought her a pair of gardening gloves. She said thank you politely in her sweetest southern lady voice, but she never wore them. Later, she told me she needed to feel the soil sink beneath her skin so the ground and the plants could speak to her. A human with such talents to connect with the earth? How'd the Fates grant someone like her to a fuckup like me?

A more heartbreaking thought hits me. What if I'm wrong? What if the connection to all these murders is *me*?

"I would never have willingly brought the attention of anyone violent to you and your family," I promise her. "Or your Fury sister. Or Poppy the..." I bite off *pig* and go with the more formal "shifter sow."

"I know," she says quietly. "Or Lowell. Or anyone else. You wouldn't hurt us. According to Stone, no alpha would harm the innocent. It's not in your nature."

My nature. She only knows part of my nature. The man. The wolf. Not the fox—that sneaky bastard who like my alpha father would have no problem killing just for the thrill, making chaos simply because he could, and lying to serve himself. Lies haven't helped me any. Maybe it's time I try the truth. "I wasn't meant to be the next alpha of the Nashville pack. Lowell was."

"Because your father disowned you as punishment for you choosing the wolf marshals over the pack." She recites the excuse that Lowell and my family told everyone. Her pretty emerald gaze flashes, and I wonder if she's mad on my behalf. It'd be nice, but I can't read the multitude of colors coming off her well enough to know what she's thinking—not with the mating bond incomplete.

I *need* her to pick me as her mate, and I can't ask her for that until I'm willing to be completely honest with her. "Lowell and I didn't share the same father, Sadie."

The fierce anger drops from her. "What?"

"It's a secret that we kept to protect our mother, but at home? It didn't matter. I served as the whipping boy for whatever pissed the alpha off. He couldn't risk leaving our mom and cutting off his connections to her family since they're practically wolf royalty. But he could take his rage out on me."

She stalks toward me, her gaze sparking. "For something that wasn't your fault."

"He didn't care. He knew he couldn't leave marks on her, and he didn't want to start a war with my real father."

"You were just a kid."

"I was a bastard and a threat to his rule. If he couldn't keep his own woman in line, how could he run a pack?"

"Why didn't your real dad intervene to protect you?" she asks.

"He already had enough heirs that he didn't need me as a spare."

"Your real dad was an alpha as well?"

"But not a wolf."

"I've seen your shifted form. You're a wolf, the same as Lowell was, except bigger and copper to his black." Suspicion lurks in her eyes along with something else.

"Mom's wolf royalty. It can cover a host of sins including paternity. Of course it didn't keep her mouth shut when she wanted to use her infidelity as a weapon against her husband."

"You're mom's a bitch."

"Literally." My chuckle seems to reel her in. She touches my chest, trailing her fingertips along my sternum, and I resist the urge to pull her to me because I recognize that deeper emotion coming off her in curling ribbons of blue—sadness. "I don't want your pity."

"What do you want?"

Truth. I can't win her until I trust her with everything. "You."

"The marshals don't know about your real dad?" She skirts the real issue between us, and I let her.

"No. If the marshals knew, they'd either fire me or kill me. They don't tolerate non-wolves. I'm trusting you not to tell them."

She sucks in a breath. "Who else have you told this secret? Besides me?" She's good. Like a targeted missile, she focuses on what really matters to shatter me if she decides to.

"No one. Lowell knew of course. He swore he didn't tell—not even Hazel."

"Then why tell me?"

The human part of me shuts down, refusing to confide the rest when she could hurt me so brutally with the information, but the wolf and even my fox agree that she has to feel some of the connection between us. "Because we're mates. We always have been or at least since your fifteenth birthday."

She curls her mouth into a slow smirk. "Drove you mad, didn't it?"

"Out of my fucking mind." I hesitate but she's not running or screaming, and damn it, by the sparkle in her eyes, she *knows*. "In one day, you went from being a little sister to the woman I couldn't stop thinking about while you still looked like a kid."

"Which is why you were such a jerk to me?" She raises an eyebrow, daring me to disagree.

"Which is why I was such a jerk," I mumble. Gods, I hate this truth-telling business.

"That explains the first three years until I turned eighteen." She crosses her arms over her perfect breasts, revealing a sliver of cleavage below her collar, and my gaze lasers in on it. "So what about the next four years?"

"Huh?" Yep. Sadie's tits render me stupid.

"Up here, Nolan." She circles her fingers in front of her face. "I wasn't a kid forever, and you didn't come courting—to use what my parents called Lowell and Hazel dating even after their engagement. Instead, you became an even bigger asshole."

"Yeah, I did." Anger builds in me.

Anger at myself.

Anger at the situation.

Anger at everything and everyone except Sadie.

"Why?" She poke, poke, pokes like she means to unravel me, to undo me the same as she unleashes her magic whip. "Why treat me like I meant nothing to you?"

"Lowell was already mated to your sister, and he was supposed to be the next alpha. They were destined to rule the wolf pack together. I couldn't screw stuff up for my brother or you and your family."

"And you didn't think to give me a say in the decision?"

"I handled it for both of us by keeping my hands to myself and your attention off me as anything but a soon-to-be relative that you didn't want. Without a kiss, you wouldn't have known we were mates. You were safer not knowing."

"That wasn't your call to make."

"But I did it anyway."

"Because you're a man or because you're a big bad wolf and whatever else you might be?" She gets in my face. "Why, Nolan?"

"Because I didn't deserve you. Still don't. I'm not worthy of being a marshal or your mate when I couldn't keep you safe."

"But you love me." She punctuates each word with a jab of her fingernail into my chest.

The answer explodes out of me. "Yes, damnit."

Sadie snatches my Stetson off my head, plops it on her own, and shoots me a siren's smile. "Prove it."

16

SADIE

Nolan Bankston loves me. Sure, it took maneuvering to get him to admit it, but he did, and he's mine—at least for the moment. Except I asked him to prove it and now he's staring at me as if he can't decide whether to kiss me or try to spank me. I might be up for either, and isn't that an unexpected surprise? He's just full of them this evening.

I tip back his hat against the crown of my head, aiming for classic gunslinger swagger despite the fact the thing's three sizes too big for me. "What's it gonna be, marshal?"

"You look good in my hat." His voice comes out rough, sending shivers through me even as I go warm everywhere his gaze lingers. Yet he doesn't touch me. Why isn't he touching me?

My confidence wobbles, and I slam my showtime sass into place as much as I would on the roller derby track. "I look good in everything."

He strokes a hand along my arm, brushing over the goose-bumps that prickle my skin. "I bet you look better in nothing."

Damn him and his sexiness. "Ooh, I walked right into that little trap, didn't I?"

"No more than you herded me into yours. Well played,

princess." He sugarcoats the nickname so it slides down as smooth as honey.

"If the crown fits." I straighten his hat, barely keeping it on my head.

Nolan lifts me against him, and the sudden movement has the Stetson toppling off and me wrapping my legs around him. He kisses me, licking and claiming as though he means to devour me, and I let him. Because with him taking the lead, I almost forget I don't have much experience when he's so good at it, that he makes me feel like a Nymph's got nothing on me. I sink my fingers in his hair that the sunset has made look awash in flames and find it silkier than I imagined. It has been over a decade since I felt his other form's fur against my skin, and then it was as a kid being protected by my own personal guard wolf. I could get used to this. A mate who's mine forever.

Forever.

A promise I can't make to a marshal who won't stay, who'll leave me to return to Nashville when I'm sworn to serve in Syn City or another deity town as my immortal mothers order. The thought sobers me, and I tear my mouth from his. Immediately, the chill of losing his warmth makes me reconsider. But no, I won't risk my heart. Not if he won't choose a mate over the marshals, and in all the secrets he shared, he didn't mention giving up his badge.

"One night," I tell him. Any more, and I won't survive the fallout. One night, and I'll have a memory to keep forever of the few hours I felt cherished, desired, *wanted* by the man who won't listen to his destiny when I can't walk away from mine. I drop my feet to the ground, putting distance between us. "We can't have more than one night together."

He curves those lips that I can still taste on mine into a wolfy grin, and my racing heart sinks. Of course he doesn't want complications or entanglements. "Oh princess, I'll enjoy showing you how wrong you are." Something scarier than the storybook

I'm-going-to-eat-you-up villain flashes in his gaze, and I go hot at the thought of him using that wicked mouth of his to show me how very bad he can be. "You should know better than to challenge a wolf like that."

"What challenge?" I ask. Despite my Fury strength and magical whip, I suddenly feel like the prey to his apex predator, and damn, I shouldn't like it so much.

He tangles one hand in the hair at the nape of my neck and tugs until I have to tip my head back. There's no escaping his intense gaze. "I'll make this so good that you crave forever together."

I already do. "I won't," I lie.

His next kiss gentles, a coaxing torment that leaves me aching for something just out of reach. I chase the thrill, needing another hit of his earlier ferocity, but he refuses to give me anything but this lazy, teasing attention. He sips at my lips as though my mouth's a treat he intends to enjoy for hours despite the time limit I set upon us.

His deliberate slowness infuriates me. I rock my hips against him, furious that he won't give me what I need. His heart pounds so hard I can feel it, and I know he must hear mine. His hands roam over my body, but it's not enough. I'm empty and greedy, and it's all his fault for leaving me this way.

He drops to his knees on the ground, and I reach to curl my fingers in his shirt to pull him back to me except a swish of fabric brushes against my legs. Color explodes across my vision, golden and brilliant—an amber the color of sunflowers that begins and ends with him.

"Here." He presses the hem of my skirt into my palms, and cool air hits my thighs that can't compete with the heat between them.

"What are you—" My question cuts off on a gasp. He slides his hand over the silk of my undies, and pleasure spikes through me.

"Convincing you that once won't be enough."

I want to argue, but I can't catch my breath enough to form the words. Telling myself I should wiggle away before the sensations steal my every thought, I press closer, wishing a thin strip of fabric didn't separate us. "Nolan." I'm ready to beg, whine, or cry.

So much for being a scary Fury. A kiss from him and I'm as weak as the human girl he ignored in Nashville.

He nips my thigh with his teeth, and the bite of pain has me pushing through the daffodil and dandelion yellow haze to see him staring back at me. "Wherever it is you went in your head, don't go there again. Stay here with me."

"You bit me."

"Just a nibble." He hooks his fingers in my panties and yanks them to the side.

Oh gods. I moan at the first touch of his bare skin against mine where I'm the wettest. No one has done this before. It's exciting and naughty and I can't decide if I should run away or trap his hand there so he won't stop.

"Sweet Sadie, you're golden even here." He slides his touch through the curls covering my sex. "You smell so good, and you're soaking," he says. "Is this for me?"

I don't answer. I can't. Not with him rubbing against my folds. Not with the way he overwhelms my senses.

"Is it?" he asks again and pushes a finger inside me. I see stars at the sudden penetration. It stings yet I need to move, to seek relief or release or *something.* "Answer me." He withdraws his touch, and I want to cry. Why does he always have to be so demanding? Say more. Do more. *Be* more. The man has always pushed me.

"Don't be mean." My order loses its snap when it comes out on a pant.

"Oh, I haven't yet started torturing you with what could be." A tug on my undies, a catch of his callouses against my softness. "Such lovely panties. They'll be even prettier sliced in two." He holds up his index finger and unleashes a claw—a trick of the alphas. Light and shadow play off the sharpness. He slashes through the silk, and it flutters to the ground.

"Hey—"

His mouth closes over me, cutting off any protest over his ruining my wardrobe. Holy Hades. He kisses, licks, and sucks until I spiral into a high that competes with flying yet I haven't unfurled my wings. No, I'm fighting to stay on my feet, my knees buckling, my head spinning, and my world a glorious golden chain that wraps around us, anchoring me to him no matter how many pieces I splinter into as I come apart. Still, I hold back.

"So hot, so wet, so very tight. I've wanted you for years. I could smell your arousal, sense your need, feel your pain." Digging his fingers into my thighs, he drags his tongue up my center. "Let go, love. I've got you." He slings one of my thighs over his shoulder, taking my weight so that I can't sway, can't move, can't fall. "I'll give you what you need."

I'm so close, but I'm scared, exposed, vulnerable. "I don't—"

He sucks my clit between his teeth, and I shatter, shaking and coming so hard that my wings shoot out as if they can't stand to be trapped another second. Everything in me screams to life down to the tiniest tingling nerve ending. The golden streaks of the mating bond glow so brightly that I wonder how I'll ever go back to a world of normal colors. Doubt sneaks through me, stealing into my chest to replace the relaxed easiness I savored only a second before.

He tightens his grip on me. "No you don't," he says. "I'm far from finished with you. I'll lick at least another orgasm out of you." Pumping his fingers inside me, he trails kisses along the inside of my thigh. "Now that I have your taste on my tongue, your scent in my lungs? I'll never let you go." His deep voice ends in a growl.

"Please." It's the only word I can manage when he has me

aching and trembling. I'm not even sure what I'm begging him for, but I need *more*.

He touches and kisses me until all I can feel is heat—light, golden, wonderful heat bursting violently within me. I fly over the edge again and again, sagging against him, but he holds me up with his shifter strength as if I'm as light as an immortal Fury's feather. When he lowers us to the ground, I wrap my wings around him like I can hold him here forever.

"Still think we only have one night?" he asks in a gruff whisper that sounds more animal than human.

I'm too far gone to fight. Not when his weight is so delicious, his scent's soap and pine and Nolan, and his skin is wonderfully warm against my face where I have my nose buried so he can't see how thoroughly he's unraveled me. I hum a non-committal noise against his throat, aiming to buy some time to put myself back together. "Night's not over yet."

He chuckles a low, dark rumble. "And we've only just begun."

"Dear gods, you're going to kill me."

"I'm never losing you again." His somberness pulls at something deep within me, and I almost tell him we'll figure out a way to make the mating bond work long distance.

Except a *boom* rocks the trees around us, shaking the ground beneath us. My stomach rolls and pitches.

Nolan jerks me tighter against him and sniffs the air. "Smoke. Fire."

Another explosion goes off in the distance. Flames shoot into the air, painting the twilight with oranges and reds. "The Pleasure District. Kiva and Dottie were supposed to be there." I don't wait for the bells or for any orders, but I won't leave Nolan—not after the Huntresses locked him up in the aftermath of the last disaster.

He lifts us to a stand and strips. "I'll travel faster as a wolf."

Nodding, I grab for his shirt as he takes it off and tug my skirt down. I leave the scraps of my undies as a lost cause. "I'll fly above." He's solid muscle, chiseled chest, and strong arms. I don't have a chance to admire the rest of him as he transforms into the giant copper wolf that I've missed more than I want to admit. For a moment, I let myself trail my fingertips along his soft fur, and then I'm in the air to fly low enough that I skim the treetops while he races below.

"We're coming," I whisper. I won't lose another two sisters.

17

NOLAN

MY WOLF DOESN'T WANT TO LEAVE OUR MATE, NOT EVEN TO LET HER take flight above us. We need to keep her safe. Pushing faster through the woods, I let my beast side take control, our paws hitting the damp grass as if we can push off the patches like a springboard.

Smoke burns my nose and stings my eyes. The yellow of the mating bond gives way to the greys, blues, and blacks of the rest of the world. My view comes in wolf sharp with the bonus of my fox's night vision.

While my human half worries about promotions and justice, my other half sticks to basic desires. We satisfied our mate, carry her scent and taste on us, and now we need to protect her at all costs. But she won't leave her Fury sisters. So we run into danger instead of away. It'll take both halves of me—the beast and the man—to sort through whatever lies ahead.

The underbrush parts around us, allowing my wolf to push faster while weaving between the trees. Things grow too quick, too big, too wild in Syn City. The immortals' magic makes it a perfect playground for shifters if not for the deity daughter predators who don't want us here as more than workers.

Faster, faster. I don't need to glance up to know my mate's above. The mating connection's strong. Another orgasm, a bite, a commitment—and she'll be ours forever.

One night. My beast wants to snarl at the ridiculous idea of less than life—this life since we missed our chance in her last. We won't miss again.

Clearing the trees, I round the corner and charge into the Pleasure District. Scents of people, panic, sweat, and animals surround me. The cracks, pops, and hisses of fire fill the air.

Women with bows and arrows pull others from a burning building. They're shouting—loud voices calling out. One aims her weapon at me, and I bunch my hind quarters to leap and attack. But my mate lands in front of us, dropping a basket that smells of herbs and my clothes to the ground. She spreads her wings, blocking my view of the others until I go around her. Holding an uncurled whip in one hand, she sinks the other into my fur, and I press close, shielding her as she defended me.

The woman yells at my mate, and I growl.

"People are trapped in the hotel," Sadie says. Her attention focuses on the big building where I was chained days ago.

The top floor blazes. Glass explodes, the windows shattering and raining sharp, slicing bits toward us. My mate covers us with her wings. When she rises and shakes the shards to the ground, I advance toward the flames. Her Fury sisters pull crying people free from upper floors. Curtains ruffle out of busted glass and open holes into the night wind as if the building has taken on wings of its own.

Waves of fire rise along the brick, stone, and wood, sending pops of light and floating ash through the night sky. The bright clouds of earlier take on a sinister grey.

The grizzly braces a heavy load above his head, letting deity daughters and shifters escape beneath. The mountain lion slinks through, dragging a pup by its clothes. No, not a pup. A child. Another small human rides on his back. *There are kids inside.*

I growl at my mate to *stay* and run for the door, darting beneath the grizzly's shaking limbs.

"No," Sadie screams behind me, but I don't turn back.

The ceiling is blinding with ribbons of fire flowing as fast as a river. The sizzle of heat makes my fur stand on end. With my snout to the ground, I follow the scent trails, pushing past the caustic explosive smells and sticking to the tracks of soap and snacks. A woman farther inside the hotel yells out names as if expecting pets to come running. Not pets. Kids. The hunch has me hurrying.

In what looks to be a café judging by the small round tables and spindly chairs that offset benches sturdy enough to hold shifters, I find the first kid cowering under a table.

"Puppy," the toddler exclaims while clutching what looks to be a toy dog.

I crouch until the kid climbs on my back and crawl from table to table, following a scent trail of snot and yogurt to the next little one. Herding that one who holds onto my fur as if I'm her favorite stuffed animal, I keep going with the fire chasing us. More screams come from behind, but we can't go back. So I push forward.

A column crashes to the ground, shaking the wooden floorboards beneath me, and still I go deeper into the terror. The shouting of names leads me to the kitchen, the scents of fear mixing with flowers and spices. A woman cradles a kid on her hip with two more hanging onto her legs.

"Oh thank goodness," the woman in blue says and takes the children from me. A Nymph. She's older than most on the team with more silver in her hair, but definitely a Nymph. "These two got away from me when the blast shook the room apart."

A beam clatters behind me, fire running across the floor in a surge that has me scrambling away before my tail and the toddler on my back get caught in the flare. Flames surround us, blocking the way I came and cutting off the door. There's no way out.

Lifting my muzzle toward the blaze, I howl long and loud. I call to my mate, letting her know everything I wanted between us.

All that could be.

All that should've been.

The smoke's so thick I choke on it. My lungs swell as if they'll burst, and the air's too hot and heavy. My wolf might be out of ideas, but I'm not. I nudge the kids toward the Nymph, and coughing, I shift into human form. My sweaty skin sticks to the floor, and my body feels as though I weigh a thousand pounds when I push to a stand.

Searching for a fire extinguisher yields nothing so I turn the taps of the sink on high and aim the spray nozzle toward the flames while tugging to rip the damn faucet apart. Even when I pry the pipes loose, it's like aiming a squirt gun at a forest fire.

Ripping up the floorboards, I search for a way out, but find nothing but the building's foundation. I haul the refrigerator away from the wall, searching for more water pipes.

"You have any firefighting powers?" I ask the Nymph. "You guys come from rivers and water, right?"

"No. My mother's a tree Nymph." She goes back to huddling the kids close.

"It'll be all right," I lie over my shoulder as I continue to pull the place apart. "Help's coming." No one will be able to make it through the inferno to save us.

The chandelier in the next room makes *ting, ting, pop, pop* noises as the once-pretty crystals explode like tiny bombs. Heavy curtains that had graced the foyer, adding elegance and class? They crumple and writhe as though they've become living monsters. Flames dance over tabletops in the former café, shattering glassware and melting the silver. We're trapped inside an inescapable nightmare.

A blast of cold air cuts through me.

"Where'd that come from?" I ask the shaking woman. "And how do we get more?" Enough to put out the flames unless it's a weird death chill. I don't want to know if the white-robed Styx have gathered outside to help us cross to the afterlife.

Instead of answering my questions, the Nymph touches the curls of the baby on her hip. "Let's hope your mommy finally tapped into her power source, little one."

Frost whips through the walls, and snow mixes with the smoke and ash. The wall over the sink coats with ice and slides away as if made of water.

"Over here," voices call from outside.

The Nymph and I rush the kids toward the opening. Huntresses aim hoses of water at the hotel's exterior, spraying with enthusiasm if not experience. A row of Nymphs behind them move their mouths in what looks like a chant, and water rises from the ground to flow our way.

Sadie flies toward me, taking the baby that the older Nymph hands over and handing the child down the line. The smoke presses at our backs, but we work quickly to pass over the kids one by one until I help the tree Nymph up into the sink. Sadie pulls her to safety, and I leap from the building just as the ceiling crashes down behind us.

Another Nymph—a woman about Sadie's age—flutters white and blue feathered wings in a globe formed of ice. She drops her hands, and snow rushes over the building. "Baby girl." She rushes forward, taking her daughter from a Huntress who's treating the kids for smoke inhalation. "Thank you," she says to no one or maybe to everyone since it took the Houses working together to save us.

"What if you hadn't gotten out?" Sadie demands, holding my clothes in one hand and hauling me close with the other.

"I'm a marshal," I say, which should explain everything but from the haunted look in her eyes, it didn't cover nearly enough. I'll deal with whatever worry she has later. "Did everyone escape?" I ask, taking my clothes from her and putting them on despite the mess of ash and soot that covers me. I can't stand seeing the hurt on her face, and I don't need to risk traumatizing the kids any worse.

"Barely," she whispers.

I need answers, not the scared sadness rolling through our unfinished mating bond. "What happened?"

Sadie's Fury sister with the butterfly wings and the mountain lion mate answers when my mate stays quiet. "We don't know how the fires started, but people nearby said it sounded like bombs."

"Why were there kids here?" I ask her.

"The Syndicate held a giant pajama party for the kids of House members and staff. With all the awful that has happened lately, they thought it would be a fun time for kids and their parents. Whoever hit the place knew that some of the adults had left on a quick run to pick up gifts that were supposed to be a surprise." Which explains the sparkling paper, bows, and boxes now half-crushed and covered in mud.

"Smelled like bombs to me," her mate says. He's in human form with a cut on his cheek and ash coating his blond hair. "You have training on this stuff as a marshal. What'd your nose tell you?"

I had a few days of classroom training on makeshift bombs and arson, not nearly enough to give an expert opinion, but he's right. "Someone set off explosives. Smelled like gasoline.

He nods. "Syn City doesn't allow fossil fuels. It runs on clean tech and magic."

Makes sense. We shifters believe in protecting nature as much as any of the immortals.

"Why go after the kids?" Sadie asks, her voice small.

"Kids are precious to shifters," I say, taking a guess. "Our kind has had serious fertility issues since the Witching Wars. Except the rabbits."

As if she heard me, Bunny walks by with a kid tucked under each arm and two more hanging off her legs.

Sadie's Fury sister curls into her mate's side. "Children are sacred to the Houses too. The Gorgons in particular, but all of us really. Once we're finished with derby contracts and House obligations, we're allowed to settle down and have families if we want. In deity cities, of course, but still...the choice matters considering some of us had the chance taken away during our first lives." She glances at her man, and I wonder if all the Furies' mates suffered the same devastating loss I did when Sadie died. If so, does a new start in this life make up for it?

Shouting erupts from nearby. A group of shifter moms and dads yell at the Houses who hosted the party. Gorgons go after Mad Maes who handed out cookies laced with hallucinogenics to some of the kids. Toddlers scream. It's a general shit show, and I don't know how this place operates without any law enforcement other than Furies mean-staring everyone into submission.

"Our one night isn't going how I'd hoped," I tell Sadie, taking my hat from her.

She shakes her head, still staring at the fire.

"This wasn't in my plans," I say softly, trying to comfort her, but she doesn't look away from whatever nightmares she's seeing in the flames. Our evening had started perfectly, but with the disaster, near-death, and definite mood killer, it couldn't have ended worse.

"Tell me, Bankston." Captain Zaleski's voice comes from behind me. "What were your plans? Did they involve the investigation I sent you here to finish because it doesn't look like you're cracking the case. It appears you're creating new crimes to solve."

Correction. Things absolutely just got worse.

18

SADIE

After another long day, I head to the side entrance of the still closed Hack and Ale, where Tisia normally takes massive deliveries of beer and food. Not today. Not ever given how quickly the support to close Syn City seems to be growing. I knock twice, and the Gorgon opens the door to the kitchen. She hurries me inside and checks the alley again.

"Expecting someone else?" I ask.

She closes the door and locks it. "The marshals have been by here, your wolf and his captain asking questions about the day that the fights broke out. They wanted to know if anyone was here last night when the fire started. Devlyn and her Huntresses stopped by too, knocking over things and searching my bar and kitchen as if I had anything to do with that evil." She waves her hand as if warding off the bad spirits, wafting white smoke between us.

This smoke doesn't smell the same as that coming from the rubble of the hotel where most of us spent hours today helping to clear the debris. It's sage and sandalwood. "You're burning protective incense."

"Horrors have come to our city. We're lucky we didn't lose

children last night in that blaze. I'm no Fury destined for revenge, but I would take it if I knew who to go after for threatening those kids. Since I don't, I'll play whatever small part I can in keeping this space safe. Same as you. But they're on a witch hunt, looking for whatever monsters they can find—real or imaginary."

I instinctively pull my basket of herbs closer. For years, I guarded our family against humans afraid that our harmless and helpful spells might be a cover for something nefarious and corrupt. "What can I do to help?"

"You're already doing it. Between the two of us, we should be able to craft a spell that counters the craziness happening around here."

Which was why I stayed up all night going through my family's grimoire, researching protection spells that had worked for my ancestors and what might've gone wrong in those that had failed. I'd hoped reviewing the spells and seeing Dr. Bomani again today might trigger a memory, but all I remember are times spent crafting spells with my parents and sisters with herbs from my last garden.

I open the basket and pull out bundles of herbs. "I collected these in the last hour."

"Perfect. Harvesting in the waning moon right before the new will give us the extra boost of celestial power we need to manifest some good for our town." Using Gorgon strength, she pulls a table laden with pots and dishes away from the far wall and pries a baseboard loose. "I couldn't have them discovering my stash. It took me months to collect." She tugs a cedar box loose. "Blessed sea salt, rose petals, white willow bard, silver, and mugwort."

I lift a brow at the last. "Not just for drugging a wolf marshal's beer then?"

"Nope. It's good for warding off evil. Which means I guess your wolf isn't that big and bad after all." She gives me a naughty look. "Or he's not *entirely* big and bad."

"I'm not answering that. Here's the lipstick and lotions you wanted. Thanks for helping me test the latest herbal additions to my cosmetics line although I'm not sure what the point is if Syn City shuts down."

"The point is bringing a little witchy into everyone's lives so they can all feel as beautiful as we do on the daily." She pats her braids which we both know hold as much magic as my weapon to call when her immortal unleashes their powers. "Now tell me what you scored us for clearing and protection spells."

I point to the herbs I stacked on the counter. "The innocuous —rosemary, lavender, peppermint, wormwood, and liverwort." Unwrapping vials, I list the toxic and plain poisonous. "Deadly nightshade, hemlock, henbane, wolf's bane."

She whistles. "Let's hope whoever set the hotel on fire never finds your garden. You've warded it, right?"

"Yes. Only my sisters can pass through the spells." And Nolan. I don't mention the last because the mere thought has my face flushing with the memory of him licking between my thighs.

"Good. Someone puts a flame to your garden, and we'll be breathing the poison fumes for years."

"Only the guilty. I wove it into the wards."

Tisia goes still. "You've lost a garden before?"

"The Huntresses threatened to do it again." My words come out quiet but they boom in the silence of the closed pub.

"Destroying a green witch's garden is the same as killing a loved one." She touches my hand. "I'm so sorry."

"They murdered me and my whole family. It wasn't as if I could mourn plants." But I did. A vision flashes in my mind— blood staining my garden back home, the herbs having been ripped out and their roots exposed. A memory? I can't be sure. I haven't slept and I spent hours with the grimoire. Looks like I'll need to schedule yet another session with Dr. Bomani.

Tisia gives me a knowing look that suggests she sees too much. "Have you grieved your family? I don't mean the revenge and anger part that comes with being a Fury, but the rest of it? I know you Furies don't like to talk *feelings* other than smash, kill, avenge. But we're friends, right? Sisters in witchiness?"

A lump clogs my throat, and hot tears sting my eyes. I am *not* going to cry. For years, I had only my family. Here in Syn City, I've made a new family and each time someone else accepts me exactly as I am, it reminds me of what I've found more than what I've lost. That happiness? I don't deserve it. Not without completing the mission that's the whole reason I have this life— avenging our deaths so that no one else suffers as my family did. "Yeah," I manage to say past the strangling knot. "Friends and sisters."

"Syn City needs to survive. Otherwise, where will humans who practice the craft be able to go? The witch sanctuaries won't take them. The world shuns them. We know that better than anyone."

She's right. I clear my throat. "Here are the incantations and invocations to the gods and goddesses that I worked on last night. With that, your family's rituals, and the magic in this town, we should be able to come up with something."

"We will. I'll get to work on the first spell jars while you collect the still water under the moonlight. I'm glad it'll be you at the swamp and not me."

No one but Tisia might understand my weird connection to the sea hags. Except Nolan. He has disappeared since his captain arrived. "The sea hags at the swamp. Do they scare you?"

"They scare everyone. But then they don't bring me trinkets they found on the sea bottom like they do you."

"One time. They brought me something once, and it's all anyone remembers. It didn't even belong to me. The dagger was my Fury sister's."

She drops my share of the spell fixings into my basket. "Why do you ask about the sea hags anyway?"

"The legends say they used to be witches. Do you ever look for your family in their faces?"

Her expression goes soft. "Do you?"

"Yeah," I whisper. "My mom and my sisters from my first life."

"You can keep looking for your past, or you can accept the sisters you have and this second life." She closes the lid on my basket. "Or maybe get some lovin' from that cute wolf marshal before he heads back to Nashville."

The reminder that Nolan's leaving? It hurts. There's nothing I can do to change his mind. The marshals come first, and I refuse to come second. Which is why I need to concentrate on keeping my city safe and exorcising whatever evil has shown up this time beyond our usual serial killers, monsters, and nightmares. "Thanks, Tisia."

"Be careful out there."

"I will. Promise." I step into the alley, close the door behind me, and take to the sky.

After dropping off the precious ingredients at the House of Furies, I make my way to the swamp to collect the jars of water we need. Despite Tisia's sensible advice, I stare at the sea hags who swim close. I try not to search their grey-skinned faces looking for any resemblance to my family, but I can't help it. I don't look away even as the curling yellow light spreads along the dark waters to wrap around me, letting me know Nolan's here.

"You won't find your family with those hags." His rich, deep voice strokes its way down the bunched muscles in my neck and shoulders the same as his touch might.

"You a mind reader now?" I hope the strange mating link that shines pretty colors doesn't let him pick apart my thoughts.

"Don't need to be. The question was all over your face."

I glance up, and his intense gaze is focused solely on me. The same as he'd centered only on my pleasure yesterday...before the fire, before I almost lost him, before his job came first again.

He looks tired and defeated from his wrinkled shirt to his pinched brow beneath the cowboy hat. I'd barely had a chance to see him and he hadn't bothered with letting a medic check him when he left with his captain. Zaleski, he called her.

If that Nymph hadn't shown up with her ability to call snow and the Huntresses with a makeshift firehose, he would've died in that fire. I'd barely felt relief at seeing my Fury sisters alive, and he'd taken off into the hotel.

I've fought to ignore the fear and sadness over *what if*s all day, but they rush to the surface now. "What were you thinking running into a burning building?"

"I'm a marshal." He says the explanation as if I'm the idiot.

"They teach you to sprint toward unknown danger without plans or a strategy?" Or any thought of how the world would shift irreparably if we lost him? If *I* lost him?

"I save people. It's what marshals do."

"Is it? From what I've seen, marshals tend to take care of their own. They don't bother with the rest of us. You sure this isn't from your real dad's side of the gene pool?"

He blanches as if I've insulted him, his freckles going stark against the pallor of his skin. "Trust me. I didn't get anything good from him or his thieving, lying skulk."

Skulk. Not a pack. What kind of animal calls their group a skulk? I don't know so I ask. "What beast side could you have that would be more self-centered than a wolf?"

"No." His voice goes rough, and not in the sexy way. "If I tell you, you'll hate me."

"Doubtful. If you haven't noticed, I tend to lump all shifters together."

He scowls. "My real father's kind? They're the worst of the worst. They'll steal from you while smiling to your face. The wolves have spent decades running their kind out of Nashville."

"To control the town—"

"To keep the town safe." He emphasizes the last word, and I don't bother hiding my awful biting laugh.

"That worked out so well, didn't it? Lowell died. My entire

family died including me, all on the wolves' watch. So what's it going to be? What could be so terrible that it would make you hate that half of you—"

"I don't."

"Bullshit." I don't spill the psychobabble that Dr. Bomani could spin about childhood traumas. "You won't even answer my question. I can always call up an info hologram and ask about the skulk hint you let slip."

His lips go flat, his jaw tightening. "My mother didn't just cheat. She cheated with the fox alpha—the greediest, most manipulative asshole. And the wolves' greatest enemy."

"That sounds like the wolf alpha talking, not you."

"Everyone knows foxes are the lowest kind of predators. I thought the wolf alpha was my dad until I changed into a fox kit. He beat me until I shifted into my wolf pup form. I wasn't able to leave the house for months because he didn't want anyone to know."

The man has such deep daddy issues. I dip a spell jar into the water, hoping the elemental connection might soothe me. It doesn't. "Sounds like I'm not the only one who needs therapy."

"Me charging into the fire had nothing to do with the cheating asshole who was my real father. Let it go. It had everything to do with me being a marshal. It's why I ran into danger instead of away from it."

Normally, I'm right there with him on noble sacrifice. I'll charge into battle, do whatever it takes to defend my sisters, be ready to toss my life to the side because it didn't matter all that much. But I can't lose someone else. I'm not prepared to deal with more grief.

"What about mates?" I ask and watch his eyes go round. "You claimed we're mates. If we'd decided to be forever mates instead of just one night, would you have given it any thought before you rushed inside? Or would being a marshal always come first?"

Because it had been his priority before our *just one night* had ended.

He doesn't answer which *is* an answer.

I don't want him to feel bad because he chose children, his job, safety, and everything else in the moment when it'd been the possibility of dying while a marshal or living to keep his promise to convince me to be a mate for more than a night. But I don't want this pain and uncertainty either.

He said he loves me. The last time I loved anyone? I died, they died, and my world ended except for a promise to seek revenge. A promise I haven't kept. I'm lucky I remembered before we got even more entangled.

"The marshals have been the most important thing in your life since I met you." I keep this about facts, not messy emotions. "Has that changed?"

He looks away. "No."

"Then go back to Nashville. I've done what I can to help you with your investigation, and it's not safe in Syn City."

"But—"

"I don't want to be your backup plan, Nolan."

He doesn't disagree, doesn't argue why mates should come before the marshals. No, he turns and walks away, leaving me alone with empty jars that need filling with still water, good intentions, and emotional shields. Now, if the immortals would just give me a supersized doze of the last, I could stop this ache in my heart.

A sea hag drifts closer and snags one of the empty jars. It's fine. I have plenty.

"Your mate pick a job over you too?" I ask her.

She dips below the surface.

"Touchy subject. I get it. Is for me too," I say.

The jar drifts my way, full of dark water, dirt, and a silver arrowhead.

19

NOLAN

I MADE A HUGE MISTAKE LEAVING SADIE LAST NIGHT, BUT I panicked. She got to me reveal my fox heritage. I hate that part of me, the memories of how I suffered for being less than full wolf, and the fear of what might happen if she tells anyone. Yet in the end, she didn't seem to care about me being a mixed shifter. No, she'd concentrated on tearing into an even more crucial part of my identity.

Being a marshal has been my life since I graduated high school. It gave me purpose, and picking between the marshals and a mate never made much sense.

Most marshals have mates who are happy with their destined love's choice of occupations. Or they seem happy enough at the office picnics and parties where I see them. Come to think of it, I'm not sure those spouses are fated mates. Maybe they're just partners who work to make their marriages stick through communication or feelings or other things I'm not great at. I should've stayed and talked to Sadie despite the creep factor of the sea hags and swamp on a dark, moonless night.

Now, I've had zero sleep, I'm coughing up soot from the fire, Captain Zaleski has told me I'm useless on this investigation and probably losing my badge, and I've lost my mate. I pull out the crime scene photos from the Tucker house and toss them on the table in my cabin, desperate to find whatever I missed.

"Screwed up with Sadie, huh?" Stone asks through the screen door. At least he's in his human blacksmith form and not roaring at me as a grizzly despite the stink eye his mate gave me earlier.

"That obvious?" I stack the photos, hiding the crime scene snapshots behind a picture of the Tucker family home. "Come on in. I just got here myself. About to grab a drink. Want something?"

"Got honey beer?"

Bears and their honey. "Yep."

"Don't mind if I do." He ducks to come through the door. Thank the gods my borrowed cabin has furniture that won't break under bear shifter weight. "It's been a long day at the school with all the scared folks dropping in to meet with both our mates. Or I assume Sadie's your mate with the hound dog look you've got going." He motions in a circle toward his face and does *sad panda* eyes way too well.

I hand him a cold one from the fridge, debate taking a non-alcoholic seltzer, and decide *screw it*, if I'm going to be miserable, at least I won't be drinking bear-friendly booze alone. "She told me I need to choose the marshals over her."

"And you told her there's no choice because a mate's forever and being a marshal's a job, right?"

"Being a marshal to help people's my calling, and can't I have both?"

"No." Stone stares at me as if one word's all I'm getting. Damn sullen bears. If he was the mountain lion, I would be begging him to shut up. Instead, I'm going to have to pry an answer from him.

"Care to explain?"

"I'm not saying you suck as a marshal but you haven't solved the shifter murders while you've been here and the visiting sow shifter died."

"I'm good at my job." I can't believe I'm defending myself to a damn bear who spends his time teaching pigtailed Nymphs how to poke at things with a pointy stick. "This is the *only* case I haven't solved."

He taps a photo of Sadie's family home with the wooden sign that says *Welcome to the Tuckers. Sit a Spell.* "And this one."

"Same killers," I explain, but he doesn't look impressed.

"Your mate *died* and was granted another chance as a Fury. Why would you stay with a 'calling' that doesn't seem all that rewarding if you can have your forever love? Only a wolf would make this decision hard. Or be selfish about wanting it all."

He's as big of a jerk as I am. Worse, I think he might be right. "You see Sadie today?" I ask, no matter that I probably sound like a lovesick pup. The mating bond let me know that she'd been at the school, bringing worried colors in waves. But I'd been stuck with my captain all day until she escorted me here a few minutes ago and ordered me to sit, stay, and not screw anything else up.

"She, her sisters, Tisia, and a bunch of Gorgons used my school to hand out protection spells to anyone who wanted them."

"It looked like you had over half the Houses there from the hordes headed your way." While I'd been answering uncomfortable questions from Captain Zaleski about riots, bombs, and the dead shifter. "I guess everyone wanted some." Further proof I've massively failed at my objectives here.

"They're afraid," he says. "If painting sigils on their skin and holding charms while praying to the gods gives them hope, I'll host every House member, every human, every shifter from here to the witch sanctuaries on the other coast."

"Prayers won't stop bombs."

"Guess that's your job since you're set on being a marshal." He lifts his bottle. "You look like shit, by the way. If I'd known, I would've brought over some of Sadie's salve."

Most of the bruises from the Nymph's beating on me have

gone. I got a few new ones from the fire and trying to pull the hotel's kitchen apart. But mostly, I'm exhausted. "Smoke inhalation. Apparently it'd keep a human down for a week or so. A little rest and I'll be good."

"Your captain put you on the marshal's version of house arrest, didn't she?" He must've seen Zaleski and I arguing earlier.

"Yep. She's pissed. I got the rundown on all the ways I've broken policies and procedures starting with Sadie and ending with running into the fire. So I'm back to wearing my assigned party costume without being allowed to attend the party." I pull aside my blazer to show the star-shaped badge alongside the holstered pistol that's considered contraband in Syn City.

"Your boss out investigating?"

"She ordered me to sit tight a few minutes ago while she left here with a bunch of Huntresses to demand an audience with the Syndicate."

He grunts, and the sound could mean anything from *your boss's right in grounding you* to *good honey beer*.

We sit in silence. I don't *do* silence. Some marshals find it effective in getting people to talk. But Stone's not a person—he's a bear, and bears are stubborn. He stares at the picture of Sadie's family home as if it holds the key to unlocking this case and I've missed it.

"Any great insights?" I ask. It's a dick question, but I've had a rough couple of days when all I wanted was to get back to where Sadie and I left off in her garden.

"They destroyed her garden?" he asks, thumping his thick fingers against a photo that shows her plants ripped out, the neat rows obliterated.

"Yeah."

"Whose blood is that staining what's left of it?"

The memory of all that blood turns my stomach sour. "My brother's. Possibly some of Sadie's family or even the killers since there was a lot of blood. The human police refused to test it since my brother Lowell was the most obvious suspect."

"What about the marshals?"

"Not their jurisdiction with one dead shifter and four dead humans. Plus Sadie missing from the scene. The press turned the story into a morbid sideshow, and the marshals didn't want any part in it."

He shoots me a grumpy look. "And you stayed with the marshals despite how they handled your brother's case?"

"They're my best shot at finding the real killers. I worked night and day to solve every case they gave me until they trusted me with the shifter murders."

"Fat lot of good that's done you. You have a Huntress watching the cabin to make sure the marshals' pet doesn't go anywhere, and you're no closer to finding out the truth about your brother's death. Or my mate's. The cub our pack lost. Or the dozens of other dead shifters."

Screw this guy. "You don't know me or the work I've done. I've helped a lot of people and stopped several other deaths over the years. Not everything's tied up in this case."

"But it is for your mate. You lost your brother. She lost *everything*."

"I know that. I was there."

"You're doing a really shitty job of showing that you remember what your mate went through."

"Our mating bond's not completed."

"And who's fault is that?" He takes another sip of the beer I bought as if he's not lobbing verbal grenades.

"She didn't want me." I hate sounding whiny. Even more, I hate feeling this fucking pathetic.

"You haven't given her a reason to say yes to your mating bond. She's a woman whose life was stolen, whose family was brutally murdered, who took a chance on coming here for revenge, who got tossed into a strange world that has become even stranger. Then you come along after years and talk about being mates when you hadn't done anything to seal the bond in the years you had to have known."

"She was a *kid*." I'm practically shouting to my shifter hearing.

"And then she wasn't. Yet you didn't do anything. So why should she commit to mate with someone who's maybe half in, someone who puts the marshals over her, someone who'll take off into a burning building."

"You helped. So did the mountain lion. Pot, kettle."

He shrugs. "We have completed mating bonds, and we think before we go in. I'm not saying you chose wrong when it saved those kids, but you didn't stop to let Sadie in on the choice. You just took off."

"Because she would've stopped me. She tried."

"You have to act like a mate if you want to keep her."

"And let those kids die?"

He shakes his head but doesn't bother answering my question. "Where'd you go after the fire? When she was upset? We took our mates home to comfort them. What about you?"

Unease creeps through along my spine, settling in my gut like a stone. "Captain Zaleski needed me."

"So did your mate."

Shit. He could be right. No, he's definitely right. I messed up. No wonder Sadie didn't want to play backup to the marshals. "I should go talk to Sadie."

"I would wait until she's not with the Gorgon. She, her sisters, and Tisia left together. They ran out of spell stuff."

"The Gorgons don't scare me."

He grins a *stupid wolf* smirk. "They should. All the Houses should in their own way. The Gorgons can still magic their hair into snakes."

A shudder runs through me. "Gods, I hate snakes."

"You'll also need to figure out how to ditch the Huntress outside."

"True. If I'm lucky, she'll get tired of watching."

"Check the kitchen drawers. Most of these loaner cabins have a deck of cards. Might as well play while we wait."

I rummage through a couple of misses before turning up a deck. "Poker or blackjack?"

"Gonna need another beer."

The bear's a damn poker shark. He wins every single hand, teasing that wolves lack patience. I'm shuffling the cards when the mating bond that has been pulsing since I kissed Sadie in the back hall of the Hack and Ale suddenly goes dead. No colors, no connection, no Sadie. It damn near doubles me over. My heart kicks into my throat, and my head throbs like someone took a two-by-four to my skull. "Something's wrong. I can't sense Sadie."

Stone goes still. "There's no distress coming off my mate, and they're together."

"I've got to find her. The garden." I head for the door. "If they needed herbs—"

"Wait."

Terror spirals in my chest where there's emptiness. Worse than I felt all those years without her because now I've tasted her and seen what the mating bond might become if we both wanted it.

"I can't wait if she's in danger." I won't lose her again. Stripping and shifting, I take off through the woods. *I'm coming, love.*

20

SADIE

"WHAT DID I DO WRONG?" I ASK TISIA, MY VOICE ECHOING IN THE kitchen of the Hack and Ale above the background *thump, thump* of my two Fury sisters tossing axes in the front of the bar. "Why didn't the cord cutting ritual work? I followed every detail in my family's grimoire." Which I brought with me along with my sisters' book of shadows in case either had info we could use.

Tisia shakes her head. "I think it might've taken, just not in the form you wanted. Remember Syn City can twist magic."

"The protection spells went fine." We'd worked on them all day at the school, testing them with counter spells and attacks. "They performed better than expected."

"Walk me through the steps of this ritual again. Out loud this time instead of pointing at the recipe."

Only Tisia would think of spells like recipes with the kitchen magic she works on the daily. Or she did until the recent craziness closed the Hack and Ale. "I cleansed the space with sage, marked a safe circle with salt, concentrated on visualizing my grief going into the cord as I knotted it—"

"Did you hold your intention in your mind through the entire ritual?" she asks.

"Of course I did. I'm not a novice. I concentrated like a mofo on putting every bit of hurt I'm dealing with into that cord. Then I chanted *This hurt no longer binds* me and *I am free* as I untied each knot. I kept my affirmation positive and willed any negative away." The lingering scents of sage, chamomile, and rosemary do nothing to calm me.

"And you made sure to let go of your grief when you cut the cord? You were ready to let go of the pain?"

"You're damn right I'm ready. That pain doesn't serve me. I need it gone so I can get clear on who the immortal Furies brought me back to take out."

Tisia reads through the rituals, the variations, the notes that my mother made and her mother before her. "And you still carry the grief?"

"The same as always." Missing my sisters and parents thrums through me as heavy as Fury magic when it hits. "I don't get it. I followed all the rules." My whole damn life I have complied with rules, expectations, and responsibilities, and what'd it get me? Murdered. Everyone I love murdered. A mate who doesn't want me... The thought trails into terror. "The mating bond. It's gone."

"What?" Tisia stares at me.

"Kiva," I call. "Dottie!" My sisters stop tossing axes and hurry to the kitchen. They'll know better than anyone with their shifter mates.

"What is it?" Kiva asks, her hatchet in hand as if she'll hack away whatever problem I'm facing.

"I can't feel Nolan," I say. "The colors, the knowing that he's there—it's gone."

"You didn't tell us you'd begun the mating dance with him," Dottie says. Her butterfly wings crowd the kitchen, brushing against the ceiling.

"Come on," Kiva says with a smirk. "You could look at the two of them and know banging was inevitable."

"Have you ever lost your connection to Stone?" I ask her. "Or

Chase?" I ask Dottie. The two of them went through hell to spend forever with their shifters, but I don't have any experience with how a mating bond starts or stops.

"When I died," Kiva says, all teasing gone from her tone. "When the curse wiped out my memory."

Dottie's wings droop. "Mating doesn't simply stop unless..." She drops her gaze to the floor.

"Unless something happened to Nolan," I finish. "I need to find him. Can you keep the grimoire safe for me, Tisia?" When she nods, I head for the door, trying to decide where to start looking for him.

Kiva reaches for my arm. "Wait. Did you and Nolan complete the bond?"

I struggle not to squirm. I do *not* want to talk about the fun we were having in the garden before the fire at the hotel. "How would I know?" I mean it as an honest question about shifters and mating because I never got into my sisters' sex lives. Not my Fury sisters. Not my real sister. But Kiva snort-laughs as if I've made a joke.

"Trust me, you would know," she says.

"Stop it." Dottie waves her away. "Did you accept Nolan's mating claim while you two were doing the deed?"

Kiva snorts again. "Banging. Boning. Seriously, just say having sex, Dottie. We're all big girls here."

"I'm so glad I'm not a Fury," Tisia mutters.

"We didn't—" I cut myself off. I *am not* admitting to everyone that I'm a virgin. "No."

"Then you're not mated," Dottie rushes to say before Kiva can interject. "He didn't bite you, did he?"

My face goes red. I refuse to talk about his sexy-time nips on my thighs.

"No teeth marks," Kiva says. "He would've bitten her where everyone could see her broken skin if he was following that stupid wolf custom."

"Not fully mated," I say. "Not mated at all right now which is why I need to be going so I can figure out what happened."

Tisia holds up the herbs and candles from the ritual that I closed. "What if you severed the bond when you cut the cord?"

"You can do that?" Dottie asks. "Why would you wish away having a mate?"

"Because he's an asshole," Kiva says. "And a wolf marshal. No one wants to mate into that madness."

Oh no. I didn't erase the grief from losing my family. The magic read my hurt over Nolan as the connection that needed cutting. "Do you think he noticed that our link is gone?" I ask.

Kiva's smirk only gets bigger. "Oh yeah."

"He has to be so devastated," Dottie whispers.

"I can fix this." I think.

"Do you want to?" Tisia asks. "Maybe the ritual cured exactly what you needed to cut out of your life."

I honestly don't know what I want, but I have to make sure he's okay. "I need to talk to Nolan."

"We'll come with you," Dottie offers. "At least until you know he's safe."

"Maybe to watch the fireworks after," Kiva adds. "We should bring popcorn."

"Don't start," I tell her.

"I'll guard your grimoire as if it's my family's own," Tisia says.

"Thank you." I lead the way to the side alley and we push onto the empty sidewalk. The Pleasure District's abandoned, and I have the sinking feeling that it will stay this way. The rubble from the hotel looks so sad, a ruin of what Syn City may become.

"Where would he be if he's looking for you?" Dottie asks.

The swamp. No. I push that possibility down the list as it's still daylight and he has only seen me there in the dark. "My garden."

Kiva smacks me on the shoulder. "Tell me I'm imagining smoke over the trees."

My heart thunders in my chest. "Oh no. The garden."

"Isn't that place warded up the ass?" she asks.

"It is. It was." Memories of the wards around my family's home being breached overwhelm me, and I push through to stay in the present despite the panic. "Let's go."

The three of us take to the sky, flying toward the woods. The higher we go, the more smoke we see.

"The garden can't be the only thing burning," Dottie says.

I agree. "But it might be the most dangerous. Can you imagine either of your mates if the air becomes polluted with high-potency wolf's bane?"

My Fury sisters fly faster.

We circle above the garden, and the wolf bane's surrounded in flames stopped only by the stones I've set around the circle.

"I keep full water barrels and sand bags," I yell to my sisters. "Those should be enough to put out the fire."

"Thank the gods it hasn't spread," Kiva says. "It's like they intentionally went for the wolf's bane."

That's not what floods me with heart-pounding, stomach-turning, dread-filling fear. "Nolan." I swoop like a targeted missile toward him. He's on the ground near the tree line, sprawled mostly on his belly but twisted awkwardly, naked and unmoving.

Kiva dumps a hundred-gallon barrel of water toward dousing the blaze. Fury strength and speed for the win. "See to your man. We've got this."

Dottie heaves fifty pound bags of sand. "Did the fumes knock him out?" she asks.

"I can't tell." And it's driving me insane. "Come on, Nolan. Wake up." I pat his cheek. Nothing. Rolling him, I glance along his muscled form, and my heart plummets at what I find. "No, no, no."

A broken arrow shaft sticks out of his chest.

21

SADIE

Syn City has descended into chaos. House members barely avoid crashing into each other in flight, the bells ring until ignoring them is easy enough, and no one seems to know what's happening. The smell of smoke fills the air with explosions and fires going off everywhere at almost the same time that make the blaze at my garden look like a candle flame.

To avoid oncoming Muses, my Fury sisters and I fly upward while carrying Nolan between the three of us. He's knocked out, bleeding, and heavy as hauling a boulder because I actually care what happens to him. If I hadn't cut the mating connection on accident, I would be able to at least sense him instead of simply holding a warm, unconscious weight.

"Did another riot break out?" Dottie asks.

I don't answer because I don't know and all I can think about is Nolan.

"The forge and cabins. Head there," Kiva shouts, and we dip toward the buildings. "What the hell is going on at the school?" Crowds stand around the school grounds, and no one seems to be there for lessons.

"Nolan needs real help," I say. "We lost our only medical

doctor a few months ago." There hadn't been much need with shifters, magical creatures, and no roller derby. "My herbal salves won't touch an arrow wound." It's like a stabbing with the knife still in place. We all agreed at Kiva's insistence to leave the arrowhead in him, which makes flying him even more awkward. He needs an expert with steady hands, medical experience, and a crap ton more calm than I possess right now.

"Where do we find a surgeon in this mess?" Dottie asks.

"I know someone," Kiva says. "Don't worry, Sadie. He's a shifter. They can heal almost anything. Plus, he's in good shape. Just check out all the muscles. Even Stone doesn't—"

"Fly faster," I interrupt. "Stop staring at his naked body, and concentrate on getting him to safety so a surgeon can treat him."

We hit the ground, and it's anything but a smooth landing.

Stone rushes forward to help us. "What happened?"

"Someone shot him with an arrow," I answer.

"A silver arrowhead?" he asks, glancing at Kiva's wings.

"Don't know." The lump in my throat burns. Damnit, I cannot cry right now. "It's still inside him."

He helps us get Nolan inside the cabin that the Syndicate loaned him as a marshal. Weird, his captain isn't staying in one of the cabins. I push the thought aside and focus on getting Nolan flat on the floor since Stone suggests it's the best place.

Kiva kisses her mate's cheek. "Come on, Dottie. Let's get the only person in town who can treat this. I just hope she's sober enough."

I don't have time to ask questions as they're flying out the door. Stone brings blankets and boils hot water. "You seem to have experience with this kind of thing," I tell him.

"Our pack lived in the middle of nowhere. We learned basic first aid and medic skills." Which explains why Kiva knew to leave the arrowhead in and how to position Nolan for the flight.

"I thought we were backwards here without police and a fire department. We need to work on getting fire fighters if the Syndicate doesn't shut us down." I'm rambling because it's better than sobbing over Nolan as I keep pressure on the wound.

"About that," Stone says. "It's not looking good for the future of Syn City. Whoever bombed the hotel? According to people seeking shelter at the school right now, they just hit the House of Muses, House of Nymphs, and House of Furies."

"What?" I flinch because I'm trained to immediately go to the House of Furies if it comes under any kind of attack, but I can't leave Nolan.

"The Furies have it handled. Your coach told the retired Furies to stay put in the staff quarters and homes. You can't help them, and he needs you now."

"I'm not sure about that." I duck my head. "He picked the marshals over me."

"Because he's trying to think with wolf brain which runs at idiot pace, but he took off to find you the second your mating bond faltered. They're usually so damn *screw the world* selfish yet he panicked at the thought of losing you. That's how a mate's supposed to act. It was his instinct kicking in."

"And it got him shot." *I* was the reason he was there. My botched spell got him into this mess. Guilt slams into me.

"Can you read anything coming off him?" Stone asks.

"No. I accidentally severed our mating connection."

Stone blinks at me with his dark bear eyes. "How? I didn't think that was possible."

"I asked the magic to stop my hurt, and *poof*, no more pretty colors."

"Because he was being a dumbass and not treating you as a mate should. Maybe he'll learn a lesson from this."

"If he lives," I whisper.

"He'll live. Wolves are stubborn like that."

I don't mention Nolan's other animal. No one knows, and I'm keeping it that way. Besides, foxes are supposed to be smart and good at surviving, right? "Don't die on me," I tell him.

The few minutes that Kiva and Dottie are gone crawl by like an eternity. When they return with a Mad Mae in tow, I almost drop my hold on Nolan's chest to block the woman.

"No. No way," I say. "You're not drugging him up with anything."

The Mad Mae grins at me, the lines around her dark eyes deepening. "You'll change your mind when he starts screaming. A little pain relief never hurt anyone."

"Why bring her here?" I ask Kiva through clenched teeth.

The Mad Mae answers instead. "I'm Galena, and I was a trauma surgeon for decades before being converted as a maenad." She gestures to her face. "The change was kind to me. Alcohol can be very preserving." Which means the woman's probably pushing seventy or eighty instead of the forty she appears to be. "I'm his best chance at surviving. And you are?"

"His mate," I answer. Nolan and I can figure out specifics and semantics later. *After* he's healed.

"Excellent." She opens one of several pendants on a long chain around her neck. "A pain killer to ease the process. Nothing you wouldn't have grown in your garden with the botanicals you use in your cosmetics."

I nod, keeping my mouth shut since the woman knew exactly who I was before she asked. *Damn maenads.* If being Nolan's mate means I can get him some care and relief, I'll be that for him.

Galena dumps the powder in his mouth. "It'll dissolve in seconds and start working soon after."

Kiva presses close. "We have a bunch of people at the school seeking shelter from the bombs. With the hotel gone, we'll need to find them somewhere to go. Yell if you need us, okay?"

"All right." I glance at her. "I can't lose him," I whisper. "I don't like him all the time, but—"

"We're here for you," she says. "He will be too. Have a little faith in the mating bond. It worked for me and Dottie."

"Okay," I tell her, not mentioning my messing the whole

mating connection up. One problem at a time. She, Dottie, and Stone head out with reminders to shout and they'll come running.

Galena gets close to Nolan's wound, inspecting it. "Smart to leave the arrowhead in. He would've died if you'd forced it out in the field." She tugs a device out of her pocket and runs it over his chest.

"What's that?" I ask her.

"Portable scanner. I would've given anything for one of these in the ER where I worked. This will tell us whether we push the arrowhead through or extract it. And if it hit the lungs."

"If it did?" My voice wobbles.

"Then he dies." She doesn't sound as if she cares either way, but she keeps running the scanner around the arrowhead, studying the screen as if it holds answers. "The arrowhead went deep enough we can push it through. He's lucky. It hit no major organs. We stitch him up and he should be fine." She stands and goes to the sink, washes her hands, and rummages for clean dish cloths. "Did you hear another bomb was found at our mansion?"

"No. Are you okay? Is your House all right?" Dear gods, what happened today? Who hates our city this much?

She lifts a shoulder. "One of my sisters found it and took it apart like a kid tearing into a toaster oven to see how it works. It's good not to be sane." Unrolling a clutch of tools, she tips her head toward my hands. "You're doing fine. Keep pressure on there until I tell you to move."

"And then?"

"Do exactly as I say. I'll need your Fury speed and strength. Also, don't vomit."

My stomach lurches. "What?"

The next few minutes pass in a blur that I would rather forget. She drags a scalpel near the entry point to make an incision and then has me shove the arrow through without breaking the shaft. Her precise instructions make me wonder how many times she has done this before. She stitches him shut, runs the scanner over him a few more times, helps me get him into bed, and declares she has done all she can.

"Here's what came out of him in case he wants it as a souvenir." She drops a silver arrowhead into my palm, and my blood goes icy cold. "He'll be unconscious until his shifter side heals him. Keep him still, don't shag him until he's better, and dose him as needed for the pain." Packing her supplies, she leaves a vial on the nightstand.

"What if we need you?" I ask.

"The whole damn city just exploded. Everyone needs me." Galena stops at the door and glances over her shoulder. "But if you two are ever interested in a three-way, call me."

I sit by Nolan's bed, waiting for a change, but he sleeps through my sisters checking on us and Tisia coming to the door.

"I brought your grimoire and shadow books," she says.

"Oh, thank goodness. I'm lucky you kept them instead of me flying them back to the House of Furies." There have been mixed reports about the extent of the blast, but my old room was hit.

"It wasn't luck," Tisia says. "The Fates kept them safe for you."

"You played a part in that. Is your House okay?"

"The House of Gorgon's still standing. Not that it matters." She sighs, and I dread what's coming. "The Syndicate has decided to close the city—permanently. Your marshal and his captain have two days to clear out. The rest of us two weeks from the time the immortals declare our new deity city. Even the Huntresses have been ordered out."

"We were supposed to still have time." I hug the grimoire to me. Things have changed too fast. Glancing at Nolan, I feel so helpless.

A knock at the door has Tisia squeezing my hand. "It'll work out," she says. "Somehow."

Dr. Bomani walks in as Tisia goes. "I heard Galena treated your marshal," the doc says.

"Could you look at him?" I ask. "I know you're not a doctor of the physical, but—"

"I'm happy to." She moves to Nolan's side and does what looks to my inexperience eyes to be a fairly thorough exam. "He will wake soon."

"You can tell?" *Please let her be right.*

"He's healthy and strong." She smiles, and I notice how exhausted she looks. I've never seen Dr. Bomani look anything less than pressed and polished. "How are you holding up?" she asks.

"I had more memories of the day my family was murdered. Or at least I think I did. They destroyed my garden which doesn't seem important—"

"It's all important," she counters. "Considering I heard your garden here was destroyed when the marshal was shot."

"With a silver arrowhead like the one he found at my family's home and the one that killed Kiva." I don't mention that my Fury sister has wings edged in the same. "My killer's here, and the Syndicate's shutting down the city. Can you say anything to the people who rule us? You're respected here in Syn City."

"But it's not my city, nor do I worship the deities that you serve. The shadow nature of the Syndicate means the ruling body can't be corrupted, but it also means that it can't be swayed by an outsider."

"You're not an outsider. Not when you've been here for years treating every bit of our crazy."

She shakes her head. "You know we don't use that word."

"My Fury sisters and I were *murdered*. There's not a more messed up kind of trauma that a person can face."

"Your entire family was killed. I'm more worried about your grieving them." She stares at me with those eyes that see too much. "Did you remember anything else? Something that could help us work through the guilt you've burdened yourself with although it's not your load to carry?"

"The wings." I move past her to the grimoire and shadow books that Tisia dropped off. "Remember when I said my killer had wings?"

"At our first attempt at regression, yes."

I flip open my little sister's book of scribbles and sketches, and my heart pangs at the loss all over again. "My baby sister drew a shadowy figure that had the same wings." I point to them. "Like bare tree branches or bones."

"No. They're antlers and horns." The doctor's voice has a steely certainty. "I heard that a panic shout caused the riot at the Hack and Ale, and I suspected it then, but this proves it."

"Proves what?" What the hell does she mean by *antlers and horns*? Like a deer's antlers? And what has wings in the shape of horns? Nothing in Syn City, or we would've seen it by now. The Furies have weird wings, but none like these.

"The god Pan. He's here."

"The satyr goat-guy? Nolan said his expert mentioned him, but Pan's dead."

Dr. Bomani rubs her temples. "The rumors came that he died two thousand years ago, but I knew that if I just waited him out—"

"For two thousand years?" Fear skates along my spine. What *is* Dr. Bomani? And how long has she been alive?

She waves away my question as though it doesn't matter. "If he's dead, then he has followers acting as if he's alive."

"Who? None of the Houses follow him."

"Or none that we know." She looks away from the sketches. "Maybe it's good that the Syndicate has decided to close the city, if Pan or his followers have returned. He was the god of wild things, a monster who pre-dated the Olympic gods and goddesses although the stories tried to make him a lesser deity. He's against order and civilization."

"That's why he has a *panic shout* thing?"

"He thrives on causing fear as much as he craves lecherous

acts with the unwilling. The panic he inspires can easily kill. It's primal chaos." She stands. "I need to go for now, but we can talk about your memories at our next session. Thank you for sharing your sister's drawings."

She leaves before I can say anything else. The cabin is quiet again, and I sit beside Nolan. His auburn hair and freckles stand out against the stark white of the pillows. The scents of soap, wolf, and paper from my family's books wash over me the same as the steady sounds of his breathing. Watching his chest rise and fall comforts me after the rattle there'd been with the arrow lodged in him. Now, if he would only open his eyes. Dr. Bomani said some nutty things, but I have to hold onto her belief that he'll wake soon. Or else I don't know what I'll do.

Syn City's falling. A dead god is supposedly back to cause panic and chaos. My killers are taunting me by shooting my mate yet I haven't gotten any *smite the evildoer* signs from my immortal mothers that means I'll have the revenge that brought me back. Things are a mess. But at least I have Nolan's warm hand in mine.

According to Stone, the wolf ran out of here the moment he felt the mating bond fall. *My fault.* He ran to my garden looking for me. *Also my fault.* And he got shot for his efforts, likely by whoever murdered me and my family. The need for revenge thrums through me the same as any high the Mad Maes must feel.

"Why does it stink of cat in here?" Nolan's rough voice has me jerking my head up.

"You're awake."

He stares at me. "The mating bond?"

"I broke it. But it was an accident."

"Was it?"

Without the colors coming off him and with him giving nothing away, I can't guess at his feelings. He's leaving in two days. If I don't have the tiny bit of connection that the mating link gave me, I'll lose him entirely. "My spell went wrong. I meant to banish the grief I've been struggling with, but the magic misunderstood when I told it to cut out what hurts me."

He looks away. Gods, he looks so much weaker than he did. How much damage did the wolf's bane and arrowhead do?

"I'll bring you some water and food. Or pain meds. Which do you want first? We'll get you better, and then we can put the mating bond back in place like nothing ever—"

"No."

I flinch. "No to the water, the food, or the pain meds? I get it if you don't want what the Mad Mae left although she seemed to know her—"

"No to the mating bond. It wasn't meant to be."

Pain erupts in my chest, as sharp as if I took the arrow we pulled out of him. "Don't say that."

"It's gone for a reason. It's better this way."

"It was a mistake. I told you the magic goes wrong sometime in Syn City."

"The Fates don't make mistakes, not when it comes to mates." He closes his eyes, and it seems as if the strength has been sucked out of him. "We tried. It didn't work. Leave it be. At least for now."

"But I—"

"Go, Sadie. Please don't make me say it again."

I should. I want to. I'd like nothing more than to yell at him to give us another chance even if for a couple of days because those will be memories I can keep. But he looks so tired and defeated. "I'll ask Stone to check on you, and I *will* come back. You'll change your mind about the mating bond."

I'll make him, and yep, the world just got weirder if I'm convincing Nolan Freakin' Bankston that we're meant to be for whatever time he'll give me before he picks the marshals over me...again.

22

NOLAN

GETTING SHOT WITH AN ARROW LIKE SOMETHING OUT OF MEDIEVAL times hurt, but not as much as losing my connection to Sadie and pushing her away. The magic couldn't have gone that wrong—not even in Syn City. If her spell cut our bond, then she doesn't want to be mated to me. No matter what she says. I've never heard of a connection failing because of any accident, and she said our bond severed because it hurts her.

I hurt her. More than her grief over her own family's death.

She's either lying to me, herself, or both of us if she thinks she's ready to simply snap our connection back into existence. I won't force her to accept an uncompleted bond that she doesn't want. She means too much for that. Instead, I'll figure out this damn case so I can win her back.

Which is why I'm standing outside a temple that looks like something out of a history hologram. The House of Huntresses didn't spare any expense. They rebuilt an ancient Greek temple surrounded by steps and fronted by six massive columns. How the hell did they lug so much marble into the swamplands?

I thought temples would smell like incense or candles, but this could be the wildest forest with the scents of trees, moss, and damp earth. The scent makes me think of Sadie's garden on steroids, without the care and tending. Instead of pretty rows and neat circles, I imagine tangled vines and towering redwoods. Not white stone columns and empty spaces leading to a wide door dwarfed by its colossal surroundings.

"You lost, marshal?" Bunny's whisper-shout would be funny except her shifty movements and the fear in her eyes scream that I should run away. "You're not supposed to be out of bed. Hell, no one knew you were awake yet."

"I'm fine." It's the same lie I gave the nosy bear shifter right before I snuck away.

"I know wolf's bane messes with your brain." She shifts the box she's carrying to one hip. "But gunslinger style isn't cool in a deity town, and you have blood on your hands—literally not the literary mumbo jumbo. You look like crap, marshal."

I ignore her comments on how bad I look because everything hurts and I would rather beg my mate to let me put my head in her lap and sleep a year than be here. My stitches must've given because Bunny's right. I have blood streaks on my shirt, down an arm, and on my fingers.

At least my Stetson shields my throbbing eyes from the sun and the weight of my gun in its holster gives me a sense of security—no matter how false. I've been shot in this town once. I'd rather it not happen again.

"I'm not lost," I tell her.

"You sure?" the rabbit asks. "I can help you back to the cabin if you want."

I ignore that too. "This the House of Huntresses?"

"Yep." The word comes out on a squeak. "No shifter with any sense comes this way."

"*You're* here."

"To check on a work crew boarding up a wing of the House of Nymphs." She jerks a thumb over her shoulder toward the distant sounds of hammers and saws. "The Huntresses called for collapsible solar panels so I brought a box to leave for when they get back from the assembly." She hefts the box she's holding a little higher.

"You're not going inside to install them?" According to the talk I've heard in Syn City, there's no maintenance or repair work that Bunny isn't in charge of.

"Hell, no. No one goes into the temple except the Huntresses. It's their sacred space."

"That doesn't strike you as weird?" Sure, marshal headquarters is a secure facility, but we at least have a waiting area.

"Nope. All the Houses are strange. Come on, we shifters look like cute, snuggly woodland creatures next to your mate and her Fury sisters."

My heart misses a beat or seven. "Why would you think Sadie's my mate?"

Bunny points to her twitchy nose. "Her scent's all over you. Don't lie to me. I'm a mom. I can sniff that stuff out in a second."

"She broke our bond with a spell, but she swears she did it on accident." Why am I telling the rabbit this?

"Magic here works funny. If she says she didn't mean to, then she didn't."

"Just like that?"

"Why are you questioning her? No offense, but your mate would be more likely to hex you for not believing her than lie to you to save your precious feelings. The Furies aren't known for being nice, especially not Sadie. Although I see she painted your arm with sigils the same as she did for me and my family. Gave us nifty little charms too like the one around your neck."

So that's where this mark on my arm and leather cord around my neck came from. I wondered after Sadie left—after I made her leave. In case it'd been my last gift from my mate, I didn't dare wash away the painted marks or take off the strange necklace.

Bunny climbs the stairs to the temple and dumps the box of

solar panels on the raised marble next to a column. "Can we go now?"

"You're sure the Huntresses aren't here?" I ask.

"Yeah, the Syndicate ordered all the Houses to report to The Rink for some big assembly. We think they're announcing their plans to close the city. You and your captain leave first."

"I heard." Worse, Captain Zaleski sounded glad when she told me. I head toward the door, listening for any signs of someone inside before trying the latch. "Cocky Houses. They leave the front door unlocked."

"Because no one's stupid enough to go inside," Bunny says on a hiss worthy of a snake shifter.

"I have a hunch that I need to check out." Without anyone around. No matter how much the Furies insist that the Huntresses can't lie, I know a wave of green movement flashed in the woods near Sadie's garden right before I went down. If I find silver arrowheads inside, that's it. We have our killers. "I'll be right back."

Bunny mutters curses. "I can't let you go alone. You're worse than my kids nosing around places you don't belong while you're still bleeding enough of a trail to lead the predators to you."

"I *am* the predator." My wolf gives a growl.

The rabbit's not impressed. "Not here you aren't. Come on. Let's get whatever trouble you're determined to find over with."

"Then stay behind me." I push inside the temple. The first room reveals absolutely nothing except tiled floors, tall columns, and stained glass ceilings that dome above us. My boots clip against the marble, echoing like gunshots.

"Nothing to see here." Bunny's shoes squeak behind me. "You good now?"

"What are they hiding?" There's nothing here. I expected to have to search for clues, but I didn't think they wouldn't have *anything*. There isn't even a door leading further into the house. "Why's this so plain?"

"I don't know, man. Maybe their goddess mommy requires it. Since they're big on chastity, maybe it's a huge empty space for virgin sacrifices." She shudders. "I can't believe I said that out loud." Staring upward, she says, "Please don't let there be sacrifices here. Or anywhere."

"You always talk this much?"

"It's been a hard week, wolf. My kids and I almost got trapped in that hotel fire. Hey." She yanks on my sleeve. "Check that out."

The stained glass above us...it *moves*. Or at least the art depicted in it does. I squint for a better look, my vision still a little hazy from the aftereffects of inhaling all that wolf's bane. "Is that—Are they—?"

"The word you're looking for is orgy," Bunny whispers. "I would expect something like this at the House of Nymphs but not here with the Huntresses. The glass is spelled so those women... fornicate with animals in a painted forest."

The wild forest that I thought I smelled outside. "We can't exactly judge. Maybe the animals are shifters." I tilt my head, unable to look away.

"Quit staring at it." Bunny smacks my arm. "*Men.*"

"Fine." I scan the room again, looking for an entrance, a trap door, anything. Finding nothing, I let my beast take over. The sound of water trickling comes through, and the faint scent? I inhale, letting the sources sort themselves out. "I smell a wolf."

"Duh," Bunny says. "I wasn't going to say it, but you kind of stink. I guess bleeding out while walking around after getting shot can do that to a guy."

"Not me." I sniff. "She-wolf. And blood. Lots of it.

Bunny stares at me like I've lost my mind, but I follow the scent. It's strongest at the far wall. Running my hands along the marble, I tap in a few spots where the temperature feels warm instead of the cool stone. "There's something back there."

"Do we really need to find out?" she asks, her face doing that nervous twitch thing again.

My fingers hit a dip in the stone, streaking the bright wall with my blood. *Oops.* I step away, but with a hushed creak, a door swings open. "Wait here."

"No way. The scared bunny who stays behind always gets axed in the stories."

I almost ask her what freaky bedtime stories she's been reading to her kids, but stop. One awful mystery at a time. This room's much warmer with a fire pit that blazes in the middle of the floor, casting flickering shadows over the glass and gold trophy cases surrounding it. I circle the room slowly, resting my hand on the butt of the gun. Something feels *wrong* about this place.

In the first case, a musical instrument is propped against an ornate chalice. I have no idea what the instrument is. It looks like the ancient version of a flute or pipe but with multiple holes to blow in. Despite the pain blasting through my chest and into my shoulder, I almost snicker. *Holes. Blow.* I blame my inner fox's sick sense of humor. The stone carvings of animals in the next case look so primitive they should probably be in a museum somewhere.

I keep walking. A cave opens behind the cases, bubbling with water in a grotto that smells of natural springs. "What did they build this place on top of?"

"I don't know," Bunny admits. "Each of the Houses sort of sprung up from whatever the immortal parents gave to the deity daughters. The Nymphs have oak trees and pools of fresh water running throughout their property. The Muses have stages and perfect acoustics. The Furies supposedly have spaces to fly and fight. But this? I have no idea."

The next case holds jewelry, and I almost skip it as being more of the same except one ring catches my eye—a sparkling sapphire solitaire on a gold band with tiny etchings. Fear and anger collide, sparking in my chest like a grenade.

If I had enough light to check, I know I would find that the little carvings in the gold are wolves. I went with Lowell to pick it up from the designer. My little brother had loved that ring for his mate. The last time I saw it was on Hazel's finger at Sadie's family home while they planned the wedding. Then, it'd been stripped from Hazel. Along with her ring finger that'd been torn from her hand, a detail I'd left out when telling Sadie.

The Huntresses killed my brother and Sadie's family.

I glance toward Bunny, spying a silver tablet in yet another case that has been etched and broken into pieces—arrowheads. "We need to go." I back away, trying to shove down the shock so I can do the right thing and get the civilian out of here. If they're the serial killers, she's not safe here. None of us are.

"Uh, marshal, what's that?" The terror in Bunny's voice has me pulling my gun—curses be damned. She points to a giant statue with a shaking hand.

A stone satyr looms above the room, cloaked in shadows. For a second, I'm not sure the thing won't come to life and stomp us out of existence. I'd found drawings of the god Pan in the holograms that ranged from the perverted to the cute to the grisly. This Pan's a monster with curling horns, a raging face, and powerful goat legs that end in hooves. Below him stands a stone bowl of blood—shifter blood by the smell of it. The fire crackling in the pit shoots into the air, and sparks fly.

"We have to get out of here now." I reach to drag her along if necessary.

Footsteps rushing toward us have me pushing Bunny behind me.

"Bankston." Captain Zaleski appears in the still open doorway, her service weapon drawn and aimed at me. "A good wolf marshal would've stayed where I ordered him to."

23

NOLAN

"Captain Zaleski." I won't lower my gun, not for anything. Rage has my vision narrowing to her. Or maybe that's the wolf's bane still kicking through my system.

"I see you found a blood-spelled door," she says.

"Yeah, and I solved the shifter murders." I wait for the slightest chance that she came here for the same reason I did. Maybe she'll holster her weapon and ask questions. But that won't happen, not with her sure and steady pulse.

"Did you now?" she asks, rounding toward the first case while her aim stays fixed on me.

The way she navigates the uneven stone floor? She has been in this room before. Her scent must've been the one I followed. Between the campfire smell and the sulfur of the grotto's natural springs, I hadn't been able to pin it as more than she-wolf. Her betrayal cuts deep, twisting my gut and making the skin around my torn stitches throb an unrelenting painful beat.

I can't lose my temper—not yet. If I play this carefully, there's a chance I can get Bunny out of here alive. I move to keep my body between her and Zaleski. "If you already knew, then why put me on the case? Why send me here?"

"Who better to send than a liar who only pretends to be full wolf?"

She knows what I am. "I have no idea what you're talking about." The longer I keep her talking and advancing farther into the room, the better shot I have at getting Bunny out of here.

"Only a sneaky fox would've found the blood door. Everyone knows your royal bitch of a mom had a fling with the fox alpha."

"If that was true, I wouldn't have made it into the wolf marshals. I would've died at the academy."

She passes by the case with Hazel's engagement ring. "That would've been short-sighted."

Irritation and alarm crawl up my spine. "You don't have that kind of political pull or power."

"Perhaps not by myself, but my associates do."

I can't risk a look to make sure Bunny's still behind me, stepping as I do. A little farther and we'll be past the last trophy case in the circle. "You're working with the Huntresses," I guess.

"Mainly Devlyn. She has been excellent in negotiating with the interspecies council."

"That explains why her scent was at marshal headquarters." The puzzle had been stuck on my brain's backburner since that first night at the Hack and Ale.

"Excellent work, detective." Zaleski clicks her tongue. "Not that the detail will do you much good when you're dead. Devlyn threatens the council members with the safety of their loved ones, and they rely on the marshals to keep them safe. It's a win-win for the Huntresses and us."

"Us? This isn't how the marshals operate." I joined because it was the noble thing to do, the most honorable path for a shifter to take.

"This *is* exactly how the marshals operate. We had to clear the way to be in charge of all shifters, not just the wolves."

My head pounds, the memory of Stone's hatred for the marshals rushing back. The bear had been right when he accused the marshals of wanting to rule over every pack. This would eliminate the rights of the individual packs and their alphas. "The alphas would never agree to giving up their power to a central authority. There would be war."

"You're right. Or you would've been."

I'm almost to the door—a few more steps and I can shove Bunny to safety. "What do you mean *would've been*?"

"Your theory of the case was solid. Kill a few select, well-placed shifters in each community, and the devastation would weaken the alphas so they'd be more agreeable to our terms."

Shock ripples through me, sending the pounding in my head to thump in my chest. "The shifter murders. You orchestrated them."

"Not just me. The marshals. We worked with the Huntresses, but the marshals picked the targets. Don't look at me like I've kicked your puppy."

"You killed innocent people." *She had my brother, Sadie, and her entire family slaughtered.*

"There had to be a few casualties to put the marshals in charge, where we belong. The Huntresses get what they want for their god Pan with chaos, and we get what shifters deserve."

"What we deserve? How did my brother *deserve* to die?" I push Bunny out the door. "Run," I yell. "I'll cover you."

She sprints rabbit fast through the first room, beneath the stained glass and onto the exterior façade that had us all tricked that the Huntresses might be benevolent followers of a chaste and pious goddess, not a monster god. I'm behind her, taking a couple of return shots at the captain when she fires on us. The *boom* of the gunshots is deafening in the marble palace. I flinch but keep going.

Outside, I push Bunny to move even faster. If we can make it to the trees, she can shift to whatever her rabbit size is to run and hide while I handle Zaleski. We make it to the last column of the temple façade, and Bunny bunches her legs to leap to the ground.

A rush of air and sudden *whoosh* has me yanking the rabbit back. During my short stay in Syn City, I've learned the telltale signs of incoming wings, and those don't belong to Sadie.

"Hello, Bunny." Devlyn steps out of the trees with an arrow notched and bowstring drawn. Two Huntresses flank her. "Silly rabbit. Shouldn't have come here." She lets the arrow fly.

Instinct has me firing my gun at the Huntress before any thought of *eternal curse on me and mine* registers.

A *crack* snaps out, and a whip streaks through the air impossibly fast—faster than the bullet, faster than the arrow. The damn thing strikes both down.

"Holy Hades," Bunny whispers. "I think I peed my pants."

Sadie zooms from the sky to fly in front of us, shielding us from the Huntress. Wings extended and blonde hair flying, she looks like an avenging angel with a scary ass whip. So much for the fiery Grim Reaper blades or even the axes she hurled at the Hack and Ale. Sign me up for my Fury's brand of weaponry.

Footsteps come from behind us, and I spin, aiming at Zaleski. I can't tell if she means to shoot me or Sadie. Either way? Not happening on my watch.

Two more Furies swoop in.

"I wouldn't." The crazier of Sadie's sisters flies upside down, flipping her hatchet over and over. In clear defiance of gravity, the thing returns to her hand every time. "Shoot at us and curse everyone in your family tree." She ruffles her wings with the arrowheads as if making a point. "Give me that before you hex yourself." Yanking the gun from Zaleski's hand, she releases the magazine, racks the slide, and ejects the chambered bullet. "Got any more on you?"

Zaleski reaches for her boot, then changes her mind when the other Fury flashes her fiery sickles. My former captain puts her hands in the air.

With her Fury sisters blocking one side and Sadie the other, I holster my gun rather than risk shooting a deity daughter.

"Did the mating link kick in again?" I ask Sadie. "That how you found us?" I must be in worse shape than I thought because I can't feel it.

"Nope," she says. "Bear shifter nose followed your trail here. Just in time it seems. You all right, Bunny?"

She doesn't ask about me, but hell, she let one shifter lead her here and bothered to check on another, so I'm taking that for a win given her prior hatred of my kind.

"This was your mate's idea." The flippin' rabbit narcs on me after I saved her ass.

"I figured," Sadie replies.

Two other Huntresses walk out from the woods to flank their leader. Neither reaches for their bow. "Your wolf trespassed." Devlyn sounds pissed, but I can't see her face with Sadie blocking the view.

"So you decided to shoot him again?" my mate answers, and oh, *she* is definitely pissed.

"You have no proof." The Huntress doesn't sound as confident this time.

"They have silver arrowheads inside," I announce. "They killed you, Lowell, your family, the shifters." I look at the Fury sister who died at their hands. "The marshals picked the targets so they could rule over us, and the Huntresses acted as the assassins to satisfy their god Pan."

"Did you say Pan?" Sadie's voice comes out strangled, and she turns to look at me, keeping her whip between the Huntresses and me. Her eyes seem darker than normal.

I nod.

She glances at Devlyn. "I thought your House's mother was Artemis, goddess of the hunt."

Devlyn gives her an ugly, cruel grin. "We're not those Huntresses. We work for the great god who wants to tear down society to restore what was before—the wilds."

An awful roar shakes the building though the damn thing

had to have come from across the city. Bunny covers her ears, and I fight the urge to do the same. Shit happens quick after that.

Zaleski screams and takes a swing at Sadie's sisters. The hatchet-happy one *thunks* her on the head with the handle, and the captain goes sprawling across the marble.

Devlyn says, "Our god's calling. Gotta go."

The Huntresses reveal wings. *Wings.* So much for them being one of the only two Houses without them. Worse, those awful wings look like bones. They're the killers that Sadie's baby sister Mable saw in her visions and Sadie remembered killing her. All three Huntresses blast into the sky and toward The Rink and that terrible noise.

Pan's shout. Panic. Chaos.

Great. We're all going to die.

24

SADIE

THE REVENGE THAT WAS MY VOW TO THE IMMORTAL FURIES? MY entire reason for this second life? I've found the targets. Nolan solved the case, and delicious rage floods my veins.

"Sadie?" He stares at me. "Your eyes have gone completely black."

Same as Kiva's have. She too has waited to know who shot the arrow that killed her. "It's time to take the revenge I promised my makers." My voice sounds as though it doesn't belong to me. It's otherworldly, supernatural, and sort of scary, but with immortal-approved anger wrapping me up in its deadly embrace, this voice feels right.

Nolan doesn't freak out. Instead, he keeps asking nosy cop questions as if nothing's out of the normal. "What about the panic shout?" he asks. "The chaos? Even though I'm not feeling it."

"The sigils and charm have protected you." I glance at Bunny and my sisters who wear the same protection and weren't affected. Unlike the marshal captain who tried to go berserker on Furies. *Stupid traitor.* She'll be safer knocked out until our Houses can decide what to do with her. "I need to go. Vengeance calls." And oh, how sweet that promise tastes.

He comes closer.

"Nolan." Dottie's tone carries tons of warning. She's the only Fury without black eyes right now. She has already taken full revenge for her death. "I wouldn't poke at a Fury in blood-rage. Especially not after you broke up with her."

He shakes his head. "I didn't, I mean I did, but I didn't. Before you fly off, can we put the mating bond back? Not being able to sense you has been the absolute worst, and if you're going to face danger or death—"

"Worth it for payback on what they did to my family," I tell him.

"One kiss," he says. "Please, Sadie. Don't leave *us* like this." He steps to the end of the marble where the stairs begin, and I fly until we're eye to eye, my whip still warm in my hand.

"Try not to bite his face off," Dottie says. "Killing him isn't on the agenda."

I grin, and the sight must be terrifying with the way Bunny gasps. "That's it for me," she says in a rush. "I'm off to my kidlets before the apocalypse." She dashes away.

"Just one kiss?" I ask him, savoring the god-like power on my tongue.

"Negotiable," he says. "Like I'm hoping you'll revisit your *just one night* limit when you've finished the whole bringing down wrath thing."

"Mates?" I need to know.

"Forever." There's a solemness to his answer, a weight.

I touch my lips to his, and he kisses me sweetly, softly. Almost as if he's saying goodbye. I'll have none of that. I deepen the kiss, claiming him as my mate and pulling away to seek my revenge. I won't have that bloodlust staining our future together more than it does our past. Colors burst across my vision. The mating bond has returned—still incomplete but tangible as though a thread runs between us.

He jumps as if my touch electrocuted him. "God-level magic," he whispers.

"Did I hurt you?"

"Doesn't matter." His answer dodges my question. "It'd be a helluva way to go."

The rush of divine energy swirling around us has me gripping my whip, ready to lash out at whatever new threat's arriving. My heart thuds loudly in my chest, and the magic spiraling through me amplifies with a jolt. A static electricity crackles through the air, making the hairs on my neck and arms stand on end.

My immortal mothers. *They're here.*

Three women in black cloaks stand in a fog untouched by the sunlight. One has giant bat wings, wearing a short dress and thigh-high boots that do little to conceal the black coils slithering along her skin. The second seems to have little form within her cloak except cold darkness. The third? She created me. When she stood above me in my family's attic, I'd believed her to be a dark angel in despair. The inky black of her wings, hair, dress, eyes, and tears makes her pale marble skin look bone white.

"We appear before you and your mates, my daughters." She sounds as if she speaks with the voice of thousands blended together. "This deity city is not what we dreamed, and you are the only ones who can fix that. Your wolf has opened the door to the enemies' temple with his shifter's blood given in sacrifices to the bastard children of a dead god. You have all you need to find the vengeance you swore."

"And Pan?" Nolan asks, and I want to shush him, to shield him behind my wings before the immortals can strike him down. He doesn't hide his fear of the one with the snake-looking tattoos that move.

A chilling laugh comes from the cloaked one. "Bastet will deal with the should-be-dead god. Dr. Bomani, I believe you call her.

The cat goddess from another culture, another magic, an older time. She's an ally in this."

"Stop the Huntresses," the one with the stripper boots says on a hiss, and I almost expect Gorgon-worthy snakes to pour from her skin. Nolan backs up another step. "Rebuild the city to be the safe haven it was meant to be." She flicks a hand toward the sky. "We will send all your sisters to make it so."

"Take your vengeance," my creator orders. "Spill their blood as they spilled yours."

The immortals disappear, and a power surge hits me in the chest, a wrath that has no end. The need for revenge strips away doubts, pain, and heartache, replacing those devastating emotions with pure rage.

It's time to go.

Kiva and Dottie's mates appear at the edge of the woods. From their solemn expressions, I would guess they caught most of the show. Hopefully they can keep Nolan from heading into a battle he can't shoot his way through.

But for now, vengeance calls.

I take to the air, my sisters at my side. We aim for The Rink, the biggest building in the city. It towers above the tree tops, smoke pouring from the roof and flames shooting from its circular walls. I push faster.

The clash of magic hitting magic near the swamp's edge not far from The Rink grabs my attention. "Pan?" I ask my sisters.

"Battling Dr. Bomani." Kiva sounds as shocked as I feel about the therapist being a goddess hiding in our midst all this time. Except her voice comes out cold and crawling. I had wondered which of our immortals created her, but now I know. The cloaked one who might as well have unleashed ice from her shadows. "Who'd our immortals say the doc is?"

"Bastet," Dottie says with a *hiss* mixed into her country twang that makes me shiver. I guess the immortal with the snakes on her skin created her. "A powerful Egyptian goddess with the head of a cat and body of a woman." I stare at her, wondering what else the immortals might have given her besides the serpent sound. "What?" she asks. "My cousin collected deity trading cards. Bastet's card is a favorite of hers."

"Explains why the shifters kept saying she smells of cat," Kiva says.

I glance below where fighting and fleeing seems to be the dividing factor between those near the staff quarters. Some shift into animal forms. Others run to safety and slam their doors.

"Chaos," Dottie guesses. "Those who didn't accept the sigils and spells will regret it." Each "*sss*" stretches.

"Should we help?" Every instinct in me screams to keep going, to seek vengeance before anything else.

"Our mates will take care of it," Kiva says.

Mates. Something else I can worry about after. Devlyn and her Huntresses have to be stopped.

At The Rink, the Nymphs outside blast snow, ice, and rain at the fire.

"Doesn't feel like the bombs," Dottie says. "Doesn't smell like it either."

We zoom past, joining other Furies with rage-blown eyes in the purest revenge black. Our color has always been our strength, our pride, our bond. No more so than now. "All of us?" I ask Maizie.

"Every last Fury," my coach says. "You and your two sisters take point. We end the Huntresses now."

I swoop down toward where Gorgons battle against a group of Huntresses.

Tisia yells out to me, "About time you joined the party."

"Devlyn?" I ask her.

She tips her head toward The Rink's roof.

Coming closer, I can see the Huntresses that fight Tisia aren't in their normal form. They have those spindly wings, but it's more. Their features have morphed into something monstrous with long claws and mouths full of fangs. "You need help?" I ask.

Tisia laughs, her braids turning to writhing snakes. "Not today, my witch sister. Fly fast before you get caught in the stone spell."

I throw on speed, racing toward the roof.

"Behind you," Dottie calls. A Huntress wings around The Rink with outstretched claws.

"On it," Kiva says, hurling her hatchet.

"Go." Dottie's fiery sickles move too fast to track. "We're right behind you."

Tucking my wings, I shove upward and land on the roof, not surprised to find Devlyn carving a path through Mad Maes. I recognize Galena and send my whip uncurling before any Huntress can touch the surgeon who saved Nolan's life.

She nods at me, blowing dust into the face of another Huntress who twitches and jerks to claw at her own eyes. "Enjoy the bad trip," Galena says with a crazed chuckle.

"Get out of here," I tell her.

"Your black eyes look amazing with that lipstick. Call me." The Mad Mae drops off the side of the roof, still laughing.

How can there be so many Huntresses up here after all those on the ground? Their god's panic shout must've called in the reserves. My thirst for revenge zeroes its Fury magic on Devlyn.

I uncurl my whip, knowing it will lock on her as easily as my rage has. It catches her around the gauntlet on her wrist, and I yank her toward me. My three years of fight training take over. Gone is the little green witch who cowered over her grimoire, searching for an answer. Now, I know. There *is* no answer in logic. Only in violence. It's the Fury way.

We trade blow for blow with me knocking her bloody. Each slice of my whip or split of her skin under my punch spikes my rage. She rakes a claw over my skin, and I lose my mind because this was how they ended my sisters, my parents, me. Avoiding the fangs, I slam my fist into her throat. My Fury wrath loves the sound of her wheezing and the scent of blood coming off her.

Another friggin' roar comes from near the swamp—that damn panic shout, and the roof trembles beneath us. A chunk of the concrete under our feet collapses, and we both tumble into the smoke and flames. Up and down seem the same in the darkness, and I lose my grip on Devlyn. The charm on my neck flies off, and I've sweat through the sigils. If I can't get my bearings soon, I'll go splat on the skating track below. At least my whip will stay with me.

Stop thinking. Embrace your instinct. My creator's order in my head comes loud and clear.

I close my eyes, give in to the fall, and let my Fury gifts focus on what needs to be done. Wiping out those who killed my blood family will save my found family, their families, and my mate.

There. I track Devlyn to the roof, following her over the side when she leaps off the six stories as if that will throw me off her trail.

Not a chance.

This ends now.

I chase her and miss the oncoming pulse of magic that sends me spinning, memories of my death and my family's pain flooding my mind. Hazel running from the monsters in the front yard. Lowell shouting for her to hurry to safety. Mabel screaming for mommy. I'm slick with my own blood, crawling and stumbling from the carnage in the garden into the house. My mother yells for me to get to the grimoire. I can barely see past the red haze, the blood dripping into my eyes. Hurt and grief and terror ripple through me.

"Sadie," my sisters call my name, but I can't tell the difference in now and then, and I plummet headfirst into the swamp below. The water crashes around me, the soothing lap of waves tugging me down, down, down to oblivion.

25

NOLAN

HELPING THE BEAR AND THE MOUNTAIN LION PULL SHIFTERS APART annoys me more than it should. Probably because my mate's off battling the Big Bad and I'm stuck here pulling patrol duty instead of by her side where I belong. I'm exhausted, aching, and not in the mood to play bouncer to a bunch of people acting on chaos brain.

"How many more fights can we break up before we go help the Furies?" I ask Stone.

"You getting anything through the mating bond?"

The link she'd allowed me when she kissed me as though I'd locked lips with a magical live wire. The colors surrounding her had been the only reason I hadn't lost my sanity when she and her sisters flew away with black eyes and supersized doses of rage. "No."

He shakes his head, picking up a bobcat shifter by the scruff of her neck as though the teenaged girl isn't swinging punches for all she's worth. "I want to be with Kiva as much as you want to go to Sadie, but they need us keeping the order in what will be left of their city, and they won't like you getting in the middle of their fight." The bobcat hits him in the ribs, and he roars in her face. "Calm down before you hurt yourself."

She whimpers, sounding more emo girl than enraged wildlife.

I point a running deer shifter to safety and watch until he's locked himself inside. "Fear's making them all psycho."

"It's a powerful motivator." When the bobcat growls at him, he gives her a little shake. "Chase?" he calls for the mountain lion shifter. "You got any more of Sadie's spelled charms?"

"No." The mountain lion holds up a candy. "But Tisia left some of her *cool it* caramels, and those seem to be working to take the edge off." He holds one out to the bobcat girl who snatches it, swallows, and stops fighting.

"I'll do a sweep of the—" My voice cuts off as terror spirals through me. Not mine—*Sadie's*. The link between us goes dark, a throbbing grey I haven't seen from her before. "Something's wrong with my mate." I move to go to her but remember getting shot the last time I ran after her without thinking things through.

"What'd you sense?" Stone asks, his no nonsense tone cutting through my worry.

"Fear." I fight a shudder. "Then grey. The link between us is all static."

"Run," he says. "Shift on the way. Don't stop for anything." The dread in the man's gaze makes me wonder what he felt through his completed mating bond when Kiva's first life ended.

I race toward where I felt her when our connection went wrong, dodging the madness around me as I shift and drop to four paws. Calling on my wolf's bravery, I untangle myself from the clothing and push to go faster. The scent of fear and sweat overwhelm me, and my chest aches where the silver arrowhead pierced, but I don't care. She's all that matters.

My wolf darts through the trees toward The Rink and the swamp just beyond it, to the edge of the water where my mate sat fearlessly while the sea hags slithered through the stillness like snakes. Battle cries, the *thwang* of metal on metal, and the flap of wings surround me. The stench of smoke burns my nose and eyes.

The moss beneath my paws has me skidding to a stop outside a brawl that seems to be shielded. It's something magical, something primal, something my beast screams to avoid. I edge around it, sniffing the ground for signs of my mate. If she's in the air, I can't track her there, but down here, my animal side can follow any scent trail.

Movement in the water has me flattening my ears. Snakes hurry away from the shore, bobbing and coiling in a dash. I cringe. What makes water moccasins flee?

A sea hag swims this way, her stringy hair trailing behind her and her milky-white eyes staring into the distance. She triggers every alarm in my beast, raising the fur at my hackles. Bobbing beneath the water, she resurfaces, twisting her head almost a hundred and eight degrees toward the magical battle. The hag hasn't sensed me...yet.

My wolf wants to run, but the fox inside me? It's cunning, devious, and centered on our mate. We can sneak up on the hag and outsmart her if necessary. For the first time I can remember, I'm proud to have my fox half if it means finding Sadie and saving our mate.

Stalking closer, I let cool water lap over my paws and soak my fur. The hag goes under again, and tiny waves ripple outward in a circle from where she dropped. She comes up, closer this time, pulling someone along with her.

I sniff the air. *Sadie.* My wolf wants to growl and snap, to swim and save our mate. But my fox insists we stay still and wait. The hag hasn't dragged her down. No, she's keeping my mate's head above the surface.

Standing guard, I keep watch while the sea hag pushes Sadie the last few feet toward the shore. I whine, and the hag's attention snaps to me. I whine again, putting all my worry into it. Cocking her head as if considering whether to drown me or not, she crawls forward, tugging Sadie inch by inch. My mate doesn't move. I wade closer, licking her face. The sea hag hasn't made a grab for me—not yet at least.

I lick Sadie again, trying to wake her. She flinches and chokes, rolling over onto her hands and knees as she coughs up water. Wet locks of hair cling to her cheeks, and her clothes stick to her. Her eyes spiral with green—confusion and fear radiating off her. What happened to my terrifying Fury mate to make her cower?

I open the mating bond, hoping to glimpse the problem, but with it incomplete, I can only scent and sense that she's trapped in whatever nightmare sent her sinking into the swamp. Without the sea hag, she might've drowned. I glance at the monster who stares blankly back through blind eyes. She retreats into the swamp, leaving me alone with my mate.

I nudge Sadie's side, trying to lend her my strength.

"Nolan?" she whispers. Her hands sink into my fur, and I revel at her taking comfort in my beast no matter what led us to this. When she catches her fingers on the cord that had been long on my human self, hanging halfway down my chest, it makes sense now. It stayed through my shift, fitting on this form as easily as the other. She closes her grip around the charm and takes a long, shuddering breath. "They used my memories against me." Her voice sounds ragged. "The fear? It was too much." Her eyes blink, the green blowing out as the Fury rage replaces it.

Take it.

I force my thoughts toward her, desperate for her to have what she needs.

Kneeling beside me, she slips the cord over my ears and muzzle, wrapping it around her wrist as she keeps her hold on me. With mud, blood, and more that I can't place, she draws symbols over my fur, chanting something beautiful and mesmerizing.

"It started with you, Tucker." Devlyn circles above us. "I put you down in that attic." Her words come out guttural and wrong. You should've stayed dead." She lands a few feet away, baring fangs at my mate. The woman's unnatural.

We will end her. Finally, both my animal instincts and I are in complete agreement.

I growl and snap, feral and bloodthirsty. An overwhelming obsession with revenge flows through my veins, a wild magic thrumming below my fur. Fury magic. Impossible yet it's happening.

Sadie stands in a slow, deliberate rise that brings power circling in a loop through us both. It's intoxicating. I want to roll in it.

"It ends now," she says in the Fury voice that calls to my beast, bringing its wrath and rage as if a thousand avenging angels speak at once.

Her whip lashes out. The scents of leather thread beneath gunpowder with not a single firearm in sight. It comes from her magical weapon—a blast of Greek fire power so supercharged that it might as well be a cannon.

She catches Devlyn's ribs with a slice that cuts deep. Blood gushes from the wound to mix with the mud underfoot.

The Huntress rushes forward, fangs and claws unleashed. I snap and bite to drive her back.

Sadie brings the whip around again, aiming higher. A long ribbon of red blooms on Devlyn's shoulder to darken her green uniform.

"Bitch," Devlyn screams.

More Huntresses land. I lunge forward, biting and tearing into the enemy. Yet Sadie stays centered on Devlyn who can't outpace enhanced Fury fighting skills. The three long years of Sadie's training while we've been apart are showcased in the lines and angles of her fighting stances, the fluidity of her movements, and her complete lack of hesitation.

After striking an astonishing blow, the mud beneath my mate

gives way, and she slides backward. Devlyn lands a hit and rakes her claws over my mate's face. Sadie's hiss of pain and the coppery scent of her blood make me abandon the others and hurry to help my mate.

"Don't," she says, and the Fury voice in which she speaks has me freezing. "This is my vengeance to take."

She's right. I hate it. My beast hates it. But I can't argue with her. She earned the revenge, and I won't steal it from her. Not even when blood drips along her temple and down her jaw.

The cries and battle clangs in the distance fade. The other Huntresses come at me as if seeing Sadie bleed renewed their craze. I bite and leap and tear into them, not caring about the bruises or cuts they manage to inflict. My only purpose is to keep them away from my mate while she fulfills her gods-given mission.

Sadie and Devlyn streak through their next attacks, a blur of wings that defies shifter speed. When Devlyn gives a roar, I lose my concentration, allowing one of the Huntresses to slip through my defenses and drag her claws through my fur and along my spine. I yelp. Pain pours through me—fire screaming along the gashes as though she's poured lava inside them.

"Nolan," Sadie says, a pulse of fear thrumming through our connection.

I want to reassure her, to protect her, to help her find her vengeance, but I stumble to my knees. I'm failing her.

With a warrior's cry, Sadie sends her whip lashing out, tearing through the air above my head and slicing into the Huntresses. On its recoil, it catches Devlyn in those horrible bone wings of hers, shattering them and leaving only jagged splinters behind.

Devlyn howls, but Sadie's already drawing back her arm again. This time, it opens the Huntress's neck in a way no ordinary whip could. My Fury's magical weapon to call? It takes Devlyn's head. The sick thud of the Huntress's body signals the end of their fight.

"For my family," Sadie says. "For my parents, my sisters, Lowell, and me." A glow of divine energy shines from her—the mark of her deity-sanctioned destruction of a woman so evil she killed any child, shifter, or innocent who stood in the path of the chaos she sought. Sadie has saved us and maybe, just maybe, saved herself in the process.

I stare in awe. My woman's spattered in blood and filth, and she's never been more spellbinding. The wails that go up around us have my attention snapping back to the other Huntresses.

My mate strokes my fur, whispering quick words of magic and mystery. Powers so strong they must be gifts of her gods and immortal creators pour through my wounds, mending and healing as they surge through my veins.

"Ready?" she asks.

I bump her thigh with my head. The sooner we end this, the faster I can kneel at my mate's feet to worship her, no matter how unholy or unsanctified my adoration for her lethal qualities may be.

Sadie rips into the other Huntresses with a viciousness my beast can appreciate. With each step she takes and every strike of her whip, I move with her in a partnership that doesn't require planning or communication. This deadly dance comes naturally to us.

No thought or reason remains. There's only my mate and the final strokes of her revenge.

When the last Huntress falls, the rage goes with it. Adrenaline and magic buzz through me with no release.

"It's done." Sadie sounds as if she doesn't believe it.

Another wave of magic hits us from the terrible god battle. This one brings healing and hope instead of fear. I breathe it in, letting it settle deep in my beast's lungs despite the awful stench of cat.

"I did what I promised. I found vengeance for my family."

Sadie drops to her knees and buries her face in my fur. "So why do I feel empty?"

Because the loss never ends. My beast knows. The missing of Lowell and Sadie's family won't stop with any amount of bloodshed. The destruction of the monsters didn't cure the hurt. I curl into her, listening to her sob her pain into my fur while I watch over my mate, our incomplete bond not letting me push solace into her.

Not yet anyway.

One victory at a time.

26

SADIE

Syn City will never be the same.

A week after the fight with the Huntresses, and the smell of smoke lingers. The sound of Bunny working with her crew to salvage what they can? It jars me with every strike of hammers, shrill scream of saws, and *pop* of nail guns.

"I can't imagine how our deity town will survive." I lean into Nolan from the now open-air colosseum left behind from The Rink's partial destruction. We sit in a salvaged section of the stands, near my Fury sisters and their mates.

He presses a kiss to my hair. "Do you want to stay? Or would you rather the immortals move you to another deity city?"

"While I've only lived here since the start of my second life, it's home, and I don't plan on giving it up without a fight."

"Then it's good the Syndicate seems to be overthrown."

No one knows in truth.

The good part about a shadow government? It keeps people from knowing who to bribe, who to blackmail, who to bomb and replace. Not that anyone from Syn City did the actual bombing. No, that'd been Captain Zaleski, formerly of the marshals which seems to be a defunct organization as far as we can tell since Nolan holed up with other shifters to sort out the pieces.

The bad part about a shadow government? It operates in such cloaked mystery that its fall is more about the loss of its following than an actual coup.

"Let's hope it stays silent," I say. "The last thing we need is another war between the Houses."

Nolan shakes his head. "Not likely with the Huntresses gone."

I don't want to think about the rage-fueled, deity-sanctioned revenge battle where we wiped them out. Not today when we're focusing on the future instead of the past.

"Dr. Bomani—" I don't think I'll ever be able to call her Bastet to her face—"says that the House of Huntresses once worshipped Artemis. She doesn't know when they switched to following Pan right under the Syndicate's nose."

"Does she have a goddess line on whether Artemis will start another House here?"

"I don't know. She has been concentrating all our sessions on working through my feelings."

"About? If you want to share," he adds quickly. "No pressure."

"Grief mostly. She said the spell misfired because you can't just wish loss away without working through it." I sigh, a small release of the giant pressure that circles in me since I've learned that recovery means accepting all of me—the good, the bad, the sad, the internal scars, and being a Fury. "We talk about you some."

"Of course you do." He sprawls in his chair, his Stetson tipped down. Such a cocky wolf. But he keeps his arm wrapped around my shoulders, his fingers stroking steady, soothing circles on my upper arm. "I'm awesome."

The mating bond isn't complete, but the link's enough to let me see through his bravado. "You miss the marshals."

"I miss the idea of the marshals. Or at least what I thought they stood for," he confesses. "Hours of video conferences later, and we're still uncovering new ways they sabotaged the individual packs to advance their plan to unite us under their rule. They didn't want what was best for shifters—just what worked for a few pureblooded wolves in their organization."

"Have you told anyone else about? You know." I'm not going to air his secrets here, no matter that we're among friends.

"So many shifters suspected but didn't say anything. Since I have no wish to stay with the marshals, I don't guess it matters. Stone and the others swear that outside the wolves, no one cares about mixing bloodlines. One species comes out dominant in each shifter, and that's good enough for them."

"And how do both halves of your beast feel about that?"

"We want to be with our mate. That's my sole priority now."

"I don't...I can't..." Since the fight with the Huntresses, since I stopped living for revenge and started wondering what comes next, I haven't been able to concentrate on anything. Not my garden when I don't know where I'll be next week, next month, or next year. Not the makeup line when my best selling point was my fierce reputation in roller derby. Not my mate when our unfinished bond stretches before me in yet another way to love, lose, and hurt all over again.

"It's all right," he says. "I'm not going anywhere. The rest will work itself out." His words seem so different from the marshal who swaggered his way into The Rink only weeks ago, determined to solve the case and score a promotion with the marshals. But then, I'm sitting in a section surrounded by shifters and comfortable with the situation.

Things changed.

We've changed.

So why do I feel so stuck?

Maizie drops through the exposed roof with the other coaches. "Houses," she announces, her Fury wings flashing dark and shiny as raven feathers in the sunlight. "It is done. The immortals have spoken. Instead of bowing to the Syndicate's orders, in the future, citizens will each have an equal vote as to how we operate. As the magic-born have their sanctuaries, our city will be reopened as a safe haven for those who wish to live alongside the deity daughters. Humans will be allowed to live here rather than being tourists or mates—"

"What about roller derby?" a Nymph shouts.

"And our concerts?" a Muse yells.

"When will the bars reopen?" a Mad Mae calls.

Maizie holds up her hands. "With the Syndicate gone, the contracts to complete the required years of roller derby are gone with it, and your immortals granted you each the option to decide if you stay a deity daughter or take your chances as a regular person without your gifts. It's a one-time option so choose wisely. The rest? We will figure out as we go, but for now, let's have some roller derby fun."

It looks like it might be our final celebration together.

Tugging my skate laces tighter, I glance at Nolan.

He grins, and a flash of his beast passes through his gaze. "Go on. I'll be here when you finish wiping what's left of the track with the rest of them."

With a quick kiss, I launch into the air.

"Players," Maizie calls. "Pick your teams of five. House loyalties don't matter. Where the track's clear, you skate by standard rules." She gestures toward the massive chunks of concrete, iron, and steel from the fallen roof and catwalks that block two of the turns. "Where it's not, we fly, and you're welcome to use full contact defense moves as well as your magic. Two-minute jams like always, but we call each game after ten minutes. Winners play winners until the last team standing. Losers? You get to buy the rest of us drinks at the Hack and Ale. Players take to the track."

I grab my sisters, and we meet Tisia and Galena below.

Galena giggles maniacally, her pupils dilated bigger than if she has polished off a fifth of fairy wine. "Three Furies and a

Gorgon skate onto a Mad Mae's team, and the joke's on everyone else."

"Thank the gods she's not operating on anyone today," Tisia mutters. "Let's skate and win so someone else's pouring our drinks tonight."

"Don't stone anyone," I say with a nod toward her braids.

"No promises, witch sister." She laughs and we're off.

Wings flapping, elbows jabbing, magic dust blowing, snake hair flying, my whip wrapping around the railing to trip everyone else on the track while I pull Dottie to fly around the other teams, we win again and again. I laugh and forget my grief. The pain that has settled in my chest like a stone floats away as light as a Nymph's glow globe.

When we finish partying the night away at the Hack and Ale, a giant copper wolf waits for me. The irony of the big bad wolf shifter walking me home isn't lost on me.

Or at least to his cabin that has become my temporary home. My room at the House of Furies was destroyed in the blast, and every shop, restaurant, and spare room in the city has been overrun with those burned out of their Houses. Yet no one took his cabin after all he did to help stop the murders, chaos, and riots.

Staying with Nolan was the easiest answer. Not that I've seen him much. He is constantly away—digging through the evidence, talking to the victims' families, and coordinating with the alphas to take down the small militia that remains of the marshals.

Tension and annoyance roll off him through the unfinished mating bond. "The alphas not playing fair?" I guess.

He huffs.

"How awful was it?" I ask. He bares sharp canines at me, and I fight a grin. "You can't solve every shifter problem in a few days. You've gotta give yourself at least a month." I'm not surprised when he bumps into me, trying to knock me off balance. "Not going to happen, wolfie. After last time's drinking fun at the Hack and Ale got me a mating bond in the making, I stayed sober tonight. Not that I regret that first kiss between us because *wow*, what a kiss."

The wolf nudges me into the woods, shifting into a very naked man and pinning me against a tree. Nolan nips at my lips. "You can't say stuff like that and not expect me to kiss you again."

I wrap my arms around his neck and drag him closer. "I was counting on it."

Kissing Nolan tastes like power and possibility, belonging and endless teasing, hunger and home. *Home.* He's my home.

There's no hiding my pounding heart or the scent of how turned on I am from his shifter senses. And for once, I don't want to. "Nolan?" I whisper against his mouth.

"Hmm." He bites at my lower lip, and I almost stumble over what I need to tell him. *Almost.*

"I'm ready."

His dark chuckle against my mouth has desire firing off inside me as bright and real as Fury magic. "For kisses? Yeah, princess. I got that."

"To be yours. For you to be mine."

"Same *one night* rule as before?" His tone comes out cagey, and I don't blame him. Our *give and take and give again* relationship has weighed on him for years.

"How about a lifetime? Maybe more since I've already died and come back—"

He kisses me again—this time in a hard, bruising liplock of a claim. "Be sure. I can wait if you're not."

"I have my pain. You have yours. Those are from the past. I want *us* as my future."

"*Mine.*" His promise comes out on a growl, but I'm not scared. His beast can never scare me again. Not when he's my mate.

"As you are mine. My first, my last, my forever."

"First?" His eyes flash gold. "Gods, Sadie. You're a virgin? We should wait. I want to be gentle with you and—"

I grab his dark red hair and yank his mouth to mine. "I didn't ask for soft or sweet."

My words trip the hairpin trigger on his control. "Wings out, love, and hang on."

I don't have time to overthink the endearment he called me. He buries his face in my neck and nips at me there while moving his hands over my body as if stripping me to my underwear in seconds has become his latest mission in life. "Hope you're not attached to these panties," he says, and the memory him ruining another pair has me gasping as he tears the lace away. He smacks me on the butt. "I said wings out."

"What—"

He tosses me in the air, and I unfurl my wings, finding my balance as he grabs my legs and settles them on his shoulders so that my thighs spread wide around his head. "Remember the part about hanging on." He licks along my center, and I whimper. This man and his wicked tongue.

Riding the pleasure that sweeps me up in its wake, I hang on like he said because it's all I can manage. I can't think, can't speak, can't breathe. Heat rolls over me, and my vision goes gold and white. An orgasm roars through me, and I bite back a scream.

"Don't fight it," Nolan says against my thigh. "I could keep at this for hours."

"No." I tug on his hair. "I mean, yes, but no. I want you inside me."

He lowers me, a slow drag of my body against his that sends friction to all the right places, and I *need* him again. "Now," I whisper and writhe against him. He lines us together so with the right wiggle, I could take what I crave, but *nooo*, he holds me in place.

"Tell me you're sure, mate."

So many words. "Yes." A simple agreement I can handle. More? Not so much.

With a single stroke, he pushes into me. Too much, too big,

too...perfect. I pull the golden threads of our mating bond tight as I lock my legs around his hips. Anticipation starts a slow crawl to a second climax.

"You're mine," he says. "I will want you every single day of the rest of our lives."

Every day? I might shatter from ecstasy overload.

"Against this tree. In the bed," he says, timing his thrusts with the filthy talk that has me squirming against him. "Out of it. When you skate. When you fly. Fuck, when you uncurl that sexy-ass whip of yours. You make me crazy with wanting you. Tell me you'll let me slip inside you any time, any place our mating bond says you need me to fill you up, to make you scream, to make you beg."

I come apart, and the mating bond locks into place. He's mine, and I'm his. For all our lives to come.

27

NOLAN

SADIE TUCKER'S FINALLY, *FINALLY* MINE. FOREVER.

By losing myself inside her, I found where I belong. With her legs wrapped around me and our bodies pressed together, she's all that matters. Not the marshals. Not shifter politics. Nothing else but this incredible woman who the Fates and Furies let me have another shot at winning in a second life.

The mating bond settles within me, satisfying me and my beast. She has completed us after such a long wait of looking for something and not knowing what exactly we were missing. *This. Her.*

Guilt and doubt creep in. I took my virgin mate against a tree in the swampland—

"Stop it." She pinches my arm. "I feel what you feel, remember? And I wanted you as much as you—"

"Needed you." I straighten her clothing, not worrying about my nudity. But death to anyone who sees my mate exposed like this. "I'll make it up to you with slow, delicious lovemaking until you can't walk for a week."

"Promises, promises."

My fiery mate. I can't wait to begin our forever together. "I love you, Sadie."

She stares at me, her green eyes shining with tears although our bond shines with happiness. My tough, gorgeous Fury undoes me. "I've loved you as long as I can remember."

Her simple admission marks me as hers forever as much as our mating. I touch my forehead to hers, needing the connection. "Even when you couldn't stand me?" I whisper, needing her to know that I realize the asshole I was to her. Never again.

She gives a soft laugh. "Even then."

Months later, I still marvel at my mate as though what we have begins fresh every morning when I wake with her in my arms and each night when she reaches for me in our bed. Syn City has become my home because it's where she is.

Sadie and her Fury sisters work on making the town into the original purpose of the immortals, a place where those with magic and those without can live together without fear or prejudice. Her cosmetics brand booms with new derby-inspired colors now that the Houses skate together in splendid shows of supernatural powers and winged spectacles.

Shifter politics take up too much of my time since I've become the local liaison for the area. Dismantling the marshal militia becomes the new purpose of the Nashville wolves. Coming from another meeting about getting electricity and clean water to packs who have suffered without under the marshals, I head toward the cabin until I sense my mate's pull toward her remade garden that's ten times the size of the original.

Gone are the wards and secrecy. Now Sadie uses her natural abilities and Tucker family legacy to foster green witches from around the world who want to experience the magical properties of land blessed by deities. This garden now feeds and heals hundreds. A few workers and children from the grade school wave at me as I make my way to my mate.

Her blonde hair gleams golden in the sunlight. She kneels

with her hands in the soil and dirt streaks across her cheeks—the girl I fell in love with all grown up in the mate who I live for. She spots me and grins, a sexy curve of her lips that holds promise of teasing and taunting.

"Save the world today?" she asks.

"No more than you." I kiss her because my beast loves marking my mate in public as ours.

She wipes at something on my cheek. "I'll get you dirty."

I nip at her mouth. "That's my job." My beast wants to rip that pretty apron off her, pull her ponytail out, and wrap my fist in the strands to bend her over and take her here. But I'll save it for when there's not an audience. "You have derby practice tonight?"

"No. I thought we'd have a date night at the Hack and Ale, maybe make out in the back hallway."

Brilliant mate. "Yeah?"

"Perhaps you'll propose again." Her wicked tone makes me fight the urge to spank her right here—something we would both enjoy too much to keep it appropriate in front of the youngest students.

"You're determined to drag this out until I have to propose more times to you than Stone did to Kiva?"

"You passed his seven attempts about a dozen *no*'s ago." She laughs, and the sound has my wolf wanting to roll in it.

"Only because I know you'll say yes one of these times." After all, marriage is secondary when we're mates—bonded for this lifetime and those beyond it.

She sinks dirty fingers into my hair, and I need to feel that touch in my fur. I should spend the rest of the afternoon in her garden in my other form, soaking up sunshine and her attention.

"Maybe tonight I'll say yes." Her gaze locks on mine, full of love.

My love. My mate. Someday my wife. My happily ever after.

Thank you for reading! Did you enjoy? Please add your review because nothing helps an author more and encourages readers to take a chance on a book than a review.

And don't miss the next book of the Syn City Shifters coming soon! Until then read more from Luna Joya with WICKED CROWN. Turn the page for a sneak peek!

Also be sure to sign up for the City Owl Press newsletter to receive notice of all book releases!

SNEAK PEEK OF WICKED CROWN

Vori hoped she'd found the right sex dungeon—the one with the Hollywood mogul who had an amethyst from the goblin's wicked crown. She had less than a month to return home to that realm with the six missing jewels.

If she didn't get home with these rocks, she'd be screwed.

Because forfeiting a blood vow meant a painful death.

The mogul fed his fetish at this sex dungeon every Wednesday night. Hump night. So appropriate. As hidden as anything could be in Los Angeles, the place sat at the top of a winding one-lane road just below the Hollywood sign.

She'd taken so many wrong turns on her Ducati motorcycle in the labyrinth of twists leading up the hill that she'd lost count. She checked the address for the gazillionth time.

This had to be a sick joke.

Someone had built the pleasure club inside a massive story-book cottage that looked as though the witch from "Hansel and Gretel" owned it—if she'd been a West Coast power player into expensive kink.

Shrink the place to a fraction of the size, add legs, and it could be Baba Yaga's house. Vori's pulse raced as if she'd run an hour at her goblin fastest. With weeks left on her agreement with Baba, surely the old crone wouldn't come all this way to collect early.

No, it simply had to be another place for humans to pursue fantasies outside their considered norms. A floodlight cast a ringed halo over the spindly turrets and crooked gables. Muffled sirens blared from the silver-screen city far below. She scanned the street, looking for the mogul's car. No luck.

Leaving her motorcycle at the curb, she hurried past the cameras on the front of the house. Humans didn't know about magic, which made it too risky to hide herself with the shadow powers she'd been gifted by a faerie queen at birth.

She looked through the windows of the garage next to the house. A luxury sports car gleamed atomic tangerine. Score. She'd found the mogul. Her pulse kicked into a rhythm as fast as her celebrity-status-gets-me-out-of-tickets driving.

The front door creaked open. Damn, she'd been here less than thirty seconds. Someone must've been watching the surveillance feed. She glanced at her Cartier watch, running her fingers over the gold to calm her adrenaline spike. She was right on time for the private midnight tour. Punctuality was necessary in both of her chosen fields. A supermodel late to a production wasted tons of money, and Vori hadn't become a master thief without knowing when to show up and when to hide.

"Hello?" A petite redhead in staggeringly tall heels stood in the doorway. Her voice was a melody of naughty promises, her sweater set more suited to prep schools and pearls than pain and pleasure. "Miss V?" Names weren't allowed in sex dungeons. Privacy came with the six-figure annual membership fees.

"I'm here for the tour." Vori stepped into the light, risking the same momentary blindness as each time she strutted a runway.

"Oh." The word puffed out in a squeak of starstruck recognition. The redhead straightened another impossible inch. "Miss V indeed. Come in, please." She pivoted on those seven-inch heels without wobbling, something that had taken months of tumbles for Vori to perfect.

Taking a suck-it-up breath, Vori followed her inside. It was just a house, a nonmagical human house turned sex dungeon. Nothing to do with Baba Yaga. Still, she traced her fingers along the gold-threaded corset under her designer jacket. Goblins and gold went together like supermodels and stilettos.

"I'm Petra, and I'll be your guide." The redhead led her through a foyer that featured whimsical stained glass and soft pastels. It was inviting, unlike the depressing medieval prison vibe of most sex dungeons. "I understand your time is limited."

"Yes, I have an international flight tomorrow." To Paris for a quick promo shoot and a lead on another amethyst.

Petra hummed her disappointment and waved at a wardrobe selection that rivaled the designer racks for fashion shows. "Our dressing rooms. We have clothes and footwear for every desire. Schoolgirl, leather-clad warrior, nun—"

"Witch? Given the looks of the place, I was half afraid an evil hag might wait inside to gobble me up."

"Good thing no one believes in magic."

Oh, but witches were real. Some good, some horrible, some she counted as friends. Of course, she'd made her blood vow to Baba Yaga, the most powerful witch of all.

They walked into a long hallway, painted bright white with gleaming hardwood floors. Mirrors on the walls gave the illusion of wide-open spaces.

A huge red "Surveillance System in Use" sign was posted on every door. No way could she be filmed here. Not if she was going to snatch the amethyst. "There are cameras inside?"

"The safety of our clientele and staff is imperative."

"I appreciate the concern for safety, but with my career, I can't risk a video." As a model known for magazine spreads involving lingerie or less, she could recover from a celebrity sex scandal, but she couldn't recover from being exposed as a thief.

Petra slid closer, her cashmere sweater brushing against Vori's skin like a kiss. "For you, we'll turn off the cameras."

Ooh, a fan. This had possibilities. "But what if I like to watch? You know, watch others being taped." Their cameras had to feed into a room somewhere, and a glance at the screens might help her find the mogul with the amethyst.

"This way." Petra led her into a retro kitchen. "If anyone asks, you've never been in here."

"Understood."

Bold red appliances stood out against the white counters and cabinets. Cellophane wraps littered one table, and dirty pots filled the sink. Nothing sexy to see here.

"The monitor for our surveillance." Petra pointed to a small bank of video screens in the corner. A grainy feed showed five treatment rooms, each play space staged with kink equipment ranging from swings to crosses to cages.

Vori skimmed the scenes, stopping to note an ornate gilded throne that both tantalized and tortured given her family history. Now wasn't the time to dwell. She had to concentrate on finding that amethyst.

She didn't need to wait long. The screens flashed, and there was the mogul.

He sat at a miniature table at a child's tea set, extending his pinky over a tiny cup's handle. The innocent pose didn't match the tattoos on his hand that marked the violent crimes he'd committed. The amethyst set in his ring sparkled in the low light.

She wanted to reach through the screen and grab it. "Any chance I can ask to join in the current scene?"

Petra crowded close. "Normally, I would say no. We stagger arrival and departure times to protect anonymity as much as the fantasy. But that client might make an exception for you. Perhaps next time?"

Vori needed that stone now. She had only three weeks until the blood vows came due on her twenty-sixth birthday. The day she'd dreaded since she'd made those promises to Baba Yaga.

Find the stones. Return home. Kill the beast.

The looming deadline made her sick. There could be no more

pretending and procrastinating. Vori had two of the stones, several reasons she would prefer to stay in the human world, and no wish to confront any beast other than the one in the mirror when she slipped skins. "I can't join him tonight?"

"No." Petra's answer came quickly, definite and bitter. "That client doesn't tolerate delays." Her words tumbled out like a whip's snap before a crack that would split skin, as if a lesson of pain raced beneath.

"I see." Vori would need to be extra rough in removing the goblin stone from a power-hungry, greed-fueled man who'd provoked that kind of fear.

"But you'll come back?" Petra's pitch climbed, the earlier sweetness and uncertainty returning. "Ask for me?"

"Next time." Time was ticking. The mogul left the creepy play area with the amethyst. She needed to go after him.

"I'll hold you to it."

"I promise." Vori ducked out the back door and hurried after the mogul.

His bright-orange car rumbled down the street, its brake lights blinking a brilliant scarlet in the darkness. This was her chance. Collect the third amethyst, and she would have half of the stones in this realm. But she'd have to catch up with him now or risk losing him in the tangled twist of roads.

She hung a U-turn so fast her Ducati almost touched the asphalt, but a streak of orange ahead was her reward. The mogul rounded a hairpin curve.

Movement flashed in her peripheral vision. A massive creature aimed for the mogul's car like a missile. The blaring screech of tires had Vori braking her motorcycle to a sudden stop.

Her heart raced, her mouth went dry, and time seemed to slow as if the moment had been trapped in a horror-induced fog.

No, no, no.

The car jerked to the right, its fender clipping a guardrail and sending it spinning. Sparks flew yellow and orange. Its hood slammed into a concrete wall in a bang of crumpled metal and shattered glass.

What kind of creature had attacked? And where had it gone? The stink of smoke and rubber stung her nose. She needed to call for help, to do *something*.

She voice dialed Alexei. Her adopted cousin would know what to do. Her gasps for air almost drowned out the phone's ringing in the helmet's speakers.

"Vorishka?" Alexei's deep voice made the endearment gruff.

"I..." She swallowed past the panic knots tightening her throat.

"What's wrong?" He clipped the question machine-gun fast.

The grate of claws on steel had those knots in her throat tangling. The mogul's high-pitched shriek rivaled an operatic screech owl.

Vori rolled the Ducati a little closer, doubting the outline in the darkness. "It can't be. Another goblin?"

"Get out of there, cousin."

The creature dragged the mogul from the car, past the one burning headlight. Green skin as soft and lustrous as emerald silk spilled over curves. A slim silver band with a thread of gold circled the goblin's forehead in the same place where a giant gold one would be if Vori slipped her skin.

"She's a goblin royal like me. But that's impossible."

"Go now." Alexei used his commander-of-demon-hordes tone. "For once in your life, don't argue. Run."

Vori had run before. So much faster than the goblin guards chasing her. So long ago. In another place, another realm. Her home. Kradnovtl.

"I need the amethyst for Baba." She could shed this super-model skin and fight without losing control, without becoming the berserker her father had wanted her to be. Maybe.

The goblin shook the mogul as if he were a toy, a shiny distraction to play with, to terrify. His cries morphed into pleading.

Alexei snapped his fingers and shouted quick orders in Russian. Heavy footsteps thumped fast over the connection. He was probably sending guards after her. "Go, now."

"I have to try for the amethyst."

"No. There will be witnesses, phones, cameras. Leave."

He was right. Damn it, the man was always right. Though the street was deserted, humans could have surveillance anywhere. But she couldn't give up this easily. She straightened her shoulders and rode forward, choking on her need to run away.

The goblin's happy howl sent shivers down her spine. Shivers colder than her home realm's deepest mine. But those shivers doubled, tripled when the other goblin ripped the mogul's arm off.

Bile burned Vori's tongue worse than a witch's hellfire hex. Rolling to a fast stop, she stared. She wasn't this vicious monster. Was she?

With a yank, the goblin tore off the man's hand, the one with the ring, with the amethyst. Vori's vision swam, her breath bursting forth in shallow pants as quick as her racing heart.

The goblin shoved the mogul's own bones into his chest. His agonizing scream ended in a wet gagging sound.

Vori swallowed the sickness stuck in her throat but gasped on a strangled breath when the goblin's gaze met hers—not the searching glance of someone looking to hide. No, this screamed the knowing look of someone who'd been well aware she had an audience all along. She—because this royal's curves left no doubt —curled her lips into a gruesome grin of sharp teeth.

"Vori."

Dread licked over Vori's skin. Cold dread. Crushing dread. Dread she hadn't felt since leaving Kradnovtl.

This goblin knew her name.

But how? It'd been more than a decade since Vori's mother had pushed her through the goblin glass to the human realm.

Fear gripped her, paralyzed her. She had to focus on now, not the past, to make sure she had a future.

The goblin laughed and ran away. Her footsteps faded into distant horns and traffic. The metallic smell of blood blended with burned rubber and chemicals. Vori shook with the need to run. Not after the goblin and the amethyst as she should. But as far from her problems as possible.

"Come home now." Alexei's booming order from the phone snapped her out of her daze. "So I can see that you're okay."

Home. To her demon-hybrid cousin's house. Not to the empty palatial penthouse she rented. "On my way." She rode away as fast as she could and didn't look back.

She blasted along the grooved concrete and striped lanes of the empty freeways from Hollywood to Long Beach. She parked the Ducati in her adopted family's guarded compound and took the front steps two at a time. She hadn't made it to the top when Alexei yanked the door open and pulled her inside. He set protective wards on the house.

She went upstairs and tried to sleep in the bed her *tetya* kept ready for her, but the gruesome murder haunted her all night. How had another goblin crossed to this realm?

A goblin who knew her name.

A goblin with her amethyst.

A goblin royal who should be dead.

Hours later, she stumbled downstairs.

Alexei sat at the dining room table, an iPad under one massive hand and a delicate china cup in the other. Whatever he was drinking smelled like caffeinated heaven. "You can't risk being photographed looking like that."

Ouch. Only family or someone in her modeling agency would

be so blunt. "I'll be fine after coffee." She headed for the espresso machine.

"No caffeine so close to a shoot. Your rules, not mine. Are you going to the spa before the flight?"

"Geez, I am now."

"I sent a crew to the collision site."

"A crew from the official family business? Or from the Maronov mafia?"

"We're not mafia." His exasperated answer was one he could wind up and repeat as often as he said it. "We're demon alliances. Our family's leadership comes with responsibilities as well as benefits."

"To better organize our crime. That's what the humans call mafia. What kind of benefit are we talking about with the mogul and my missing amethysts?"

"There will be no evidence that you were at the crash site, no clues for police to conclude anything other than a rich man in a fancy sports car took a corner too fast."

Relief surged through her veins, waking her up more than an espresso triple shot. "Thank you."

"Would you like me to send a crew to the sex club to take care of any loose ends?"

Her stomach clawed its way toward her throat. "No." She couldn't risk Petra, an innocent human, being caught in the cross hairs of a supernatural war.

He studied her for a long, annoying moment. "No more tracking the amethysts alone."

"Stop playing at boss. It might work with your mob crews, but not with me."

He flipped through articles on his screen, probably combing headlines for additions to his collection of woo-woo magic weirdness. "I'm worried for your safety, cousin. You know what happens if someone breaks a blood vow with Baba Yaga."

"Everyone knows. A horrible death. I'm fully aware of the timeline counting down on finding the amethysts, going through the goblin glass, and killing some mysterious beast." She straightened to her full five feet, ten inches. She could do this. One crisis at a time. "I'll track the next amethyst—the one in Paris—and then figure out what to do about this one."

"Anything you're not telling me?"

She swallowed a curse. How did he seem to sniff out lies? "I've been over every detail of the three blood vows Baba Yaga forced me to swear." But she'd left out the part about the crone spelling the only existing goblin glass to self-destruct five days after Vori's twenty-sixth birthday. She'd need to make it back to the human realm before the glass closed for the last time, or she'd be stuck in Kradnovtl forever.

The weight of his stare might've been suffocating for anyone else. "What about your realm's laws requiring you to have a consort? Or are you hoping for an exemption?"

"Riiight." She choked out an ugly snort. "A special exception? For me? Their princess? After almost every royal was massacred by the mad king?"

"You shouldn't call him that." Alexei's expression hardened to brimstone-solid lines and angles. "He was—"

"My father. Don't remind me. I know demon law is all patriarchy pride, but I hated that man."

"You don't know that he's dead."

"My deranged daddy is definitely dead. Otherwise, he would've crossed any realm to drag me back, to make sure I birthed little golden-blooded goblins, to carry on the whole divine-power lie. Or to sacrifice me to satisfy his forgotten gods. Since he hasn't done either these thirteen years past, he's dead."

"So who would be on the goblin throne?"

"His half brother, my uncle. Which means he has the crown centerpiece amethyst I'll need for Baba Yaga."

"*You* steal from family?" The sarcasm bled through each of his words.

"Keep your wings on. I pay you back for what I steal—mostly. And my uncle Lenneck doesn't need the amethyst as much as I do. He doesn't have an evil witch counting down his days to a messed-up due date. Or maybe he's already dead."

Alexei stared as if he could sense secrets beneath her supermodel and goblin skins. "And the queen consort? Your mother?" His soft voice betrayed the way his words sliced at Vori.

Grief—the kind with jagged edges that should've been smoothed by years of doubt—stabbed at her all over again. "I don't know." Because any other answer might rip her apart.

"Have you picked a consort candidate?"

"No." How could she ask someone to put their life on the line by traveling to the goblin realm? Such a tempting offer, said no one ever. "Perhaps I'll copy the original goblin queen's power move and match myself with a witch consort."

Alexei gave a grunt that could mean so many things. "Low blow, cousin."

"Sorry. I didn't think." Shame sent a wave of prickling heat over her. *Alys.* The witch Senate had stolen Alexei's sister. Her disappearance was the reason he read every tabloid, every newspaper, every gossip site, searching for clues. "I shouldn't have mentioned witches. I know how much you hate them."

"Supremacist hags." He blasted her with his you're-lucky-you're-family glare. "I'll blame the fact you had to witness a goblin rip apart a car like tin foil and hatchet a man with his own arm. Enjoy your spa day."

Nothing she could say would fix this. The embarrassment and fear stayed with her through the drive and at the spa, twisting her gut into knots and tightening her face into harsh lines no matter how much the esthetician pinched and poked.

Her phone rang. A no-no in the eucalyptus-scented retreat,

but a rule she was allowed to break. A perk of fame. The name of the witch who'd recovered an amethyst for her flashed across the screen. Vori waved off the staff.

"Yes?" She didn't bother with small talk. Diego was a friend. But he was an interrupting-her-spa-day friend.

"Where did you get the clippings?" he asked.

The newspaper articles she'd found in Alexei's collection to replace some Diego had lost. "I told you they were copies. I stole nothing." Not this time anyway. "No one will come looking for them."

"Are there more?" Ocean waves crashing behind him underscored the gravity of his voice.

She paused, hoping he read the "yes, but" in her silence. "There are, but you won't like where they are kept." Diego and her cousin had not had a good first meeting.

"Alexei's warehouse." He sounded as grumbly as a bear shifter.

"You guessed it."

"Can you get me in?"

She needed something to get her mind off last night. Helping Diego access the woo-woo collection would be easy enough.

Hours later, he flipped through article after article while she researched the lackluster lead she had on the amethyst in Paris. Diego was famous for his tracking skills. She kicked at his chair. "When you're searching for something, what's your secret?"

"I call to it." He said it like anyone could do it, no big freakin' powers deal. Such a witch answer. "I concentrate on what I really want to find and wish it to me. But you have to know what you want first."

"Freedom."

"From what? You're living the glam celebrity life."

"From some blood vows I shouldn't have made."

Diego snapped his gaze to hers. "I *knew* you weren't human. What are you? Part elf?"

"Elves don't exist." She implied the *duh*. Anything other than admitting that she was a goblin princess because those didn't exist in this realm either.

"Oh, come on. You have to tell me."

"No. What do they say? Nosy cats end up eaten?"

He shot her a look—disturbed, disgust, doubtful. "We need to talk about who you hang around if you think that's the saying."

"We were talking blood vows." She stressed the last two words to keep him from concentrating on species.

He turned another page in the biggest book of weird. "Who'd you promise?"

"Baba Yaga."

Diego's stare hit her like a ton of goblin gold. "Damn." The word carried the weight of the excruciating hexes that would happen if she didn't deliver on the vows. "There's no wishing your way out of those."

"Maybe I could wish my way to completing one of my three promises instead. I need to find other amethysts like the ring you recovered, and I have this locator." She pulled an engraved silver charm from inside her collar, the one she wore along with an enchantment that made her gold royal blood look human red.

He whistled low. "That's a Nahualli-crafted charm. Made by a witch Senate heir, the best spellcaster in the world."

"Don't you hate the witch Senate?"

"I'm learning to be more selective in my down-with-the-authorities vibe."

"Ah, your crush on one of their Legacy heirs is changing your mind about the horrible hags?"

"No." He didn't sound at all sure. "Anyway, that charm must've cost a fortune on the magic market."

"It was a gift."

"Another marriage proposal? Do you get to keep the engagement presents every time you say no?"

"It wasn't like that. A witch gave it to me one night at a club. We'd just met."

"Being a supermodel must be tough." His sarcasm made the truth even worse.

"He ghosted me." She whispered the impossibility. Daniel Perry had left *her*. A supermodel. A princess. "I should've tossed the charm, but...I couldn't. He said he hoped the spell would bring me more luck in finding my heart's desire than it did him. He was so beautiful and broken."

"How long've you been carrying his not-so-lucky charm around?"

"Two years. I couldn't believe he was out on Halloween. For a witch, that's bold."

"Or stupid. For him to leave you, I'm betting on stupid. So are you going to try the locator spell or not?"

"Yes." No matter how much she wanted to save it. "For the other amethysts."

"Remember, it has to be what your heart desires."

"Getting out of the blood vows is all I want." She pricked her finger, touched her spelled-red-instead-of-goblin-princess-gold blood to the charm, and invoked the premade charm.

"Well, did it buzz or telepath you directions?" Diego crowded her. "What happened?"

"Nothing. Absolutely nothing." Disappointment rolled through her one nonmagic wave at a time.

Diego's phone rang. He sounded annoyed with the caller. In a flash, his expression changed from get-to-the-point crankiness to wide eyes and a tense jaw. "Vori, we need to go." He jumped to his feet and ran for the stairs.

"What's happening?" She followed as fast as she could in high-heeled boots.

"We need to rescue my Legacy love from a secret Senate prison."

A jailbreak that would piss off the hideous hags? "I'm so in."

Don't stop now. Keep reading with your copy of WICKED CROWN available now.

And sign up for the latest news, giveaways, and more from Luna Joya: lunajoya.com/newsletter/

Want even more from Luna Joya? Try the Wicked series with **WICKED CROWN** available now, and sign up for the latest news, giveaways, and more from Luna Joya: lunajoya.com/newsletter/

She's not who-or what-she appears to be. Neither is he.

Supermodel Vori would be happy to stay in the human world, blissfully ignoring her true nature. But no. The blood vow she once made requires her to return to the Goblin Court. And since going alone would mean consenting to an arranged marriage, she needs a fake husband. Someone no one would miss if there was an unfortunate...accident. Vori knows the perfect villain for the job.

Witch Perry used to be a hotshot lawyer. But that was before he made all the wrong choices, wound up in league with a demon, and was left to rot in prison. Now, he has a second chance. He can finally earn his redemption. Too bad his last hope is the woman he ghosted two years ago.

It's not long before Vori and Perry realize they aren't as different as they thought-and that the line between enemies and lovers can be razor thin. But if they want their happily ever after, they'll first have to stop a supernatural killer and survive a royal smackdown. Should be easy for a goblin princess and her dashing antihero, right?

If only.

Please sign up for the City Owl Press <u>newsletter</u> for chances to win special subscriber-only contests and giveaways as well as receiving information on upcoming releases and special excerpts.

All reviews are **welcome** and **appreciated**. Please consider leaving one on your favorite social media and book buying sites.

For books in the world of romance and speculative fiction that embody Innovation, Creativity, and Affordability, check out City Owl Press at <u>www.cityowlpress.com</u>.

ACKNOWLEDGMENTS

For those readers who told me the books had cost you a night's sleep, or you wanted to be adopted into these magical families, or you couldn't wait for the next book—this is for you. Thanks so much to every reader who spends time in my story world.

To the members of Luna's Lovelies, I adore y'all. To Laura the Literary Vixen, what would I do without you?

A big kiss to my husband. You and Tiny Editor are my world. Love to my parents for encouraging imagination and wonder.

To the BookTok community, Bookstagrammers, reviewers, bloggers, artists, and readers who have spread the word about my stories, thank you for everything. You keep me inspired.

ABOUT THE AUTHOR

A survivor of traumatic brain injury with steel body parts, Luna lives in SoCal with her combat veteran husband and their two-pound terror of a rescue pup, #TinyEditor. She loves Disney, tacos, and dragon shifters.

Luna Joya writes steamy romances that are "wickedly delightful" (*Publishers Weekly*).

The "delightfully devious" Luna writes "action-packed paranormal romantic thrillers, singing with magical power and humming with sensuality that will leave readers breathless." (*InD'Tale Magazine*).

Want to be the first to get a look at covers, sneak peeks, and more? Sign up for my newsletter at lunajoya.com/newsletter/

Want to hear about all my pre-orders? Follow me on BookBub at
www.bookbub.com/authors/luna-joya

Facebook Group:
www.facebook.com/groups/lunaslovelies

ABOUT THE PUBLISHER

City Owl Press is a cutting edge indie publishing company, bringing the world of romance and speculative fiction to discerning readers.

Escape Your World. Get Lost in Ours!

www.cityowlpress.com

facebook.com/YourCityOwlPress
x.com/cityowlpress
instagram.com/cityowlbooks
pinterest.com/cityowlpress